ALI
LOVE

Other books by Alan Rodgers

Blood of the Children
Fire
Night
New Life for the Dead
Pandora
The Bear Who Found Christmas
Bone Music
Ghosts Who Cannot Sleep
Her Misbegotten Son
Mernace: Battle Mountain

ALIEN LOVE

ALAN RODGERS

WILDSIDE PRESS
Doylestown, Pennsylvania

Alien Love
A publication of
Wildside Press
P.O. Box 301
Holicong, PA 18928-0301
www.wildsidepress.com

FIRST EDITION

for Jade, Yog, Ratz
and the folks at SFF Net.
Good friends, good comapany.

I

The year Walt Fulton turned twenty-eight he fell in love.

In some ways everything that happened to Walt that year – meeting Rick, meeting Lena, the awful stuff with the Space Pirates, even falling in love – in some ways all of it was a trap that sprang closed around him in slow motion, bit by bit by bit.

But love is always like that, isn't it? Love is a trap that we're all born needing to find, and it finds us, and it takes us, and makes us things we never knew we'd be.

That was what it was for Walt, anyway. Sometimes when he looked back on it he knew that there were ways and places that he could have stepped just one step aside and never fallen into it. If he'd made that step he would have saved himself a world of grief and trouble, and spared himself the affliction that went on to plague him every day he lived. But he would have missed something, too – something precious and divine, a thing so dear he treasured it beyond hope, reason, and the value of his life.

Traps are like that sometimes. They take us because we need them, and they need us in turn.

II

That was a bad year for Walt, even before he fell in love.

It was the year after the war and getting lost in time and eaten by Space Pirates and rescued by the Space Cavalry just before his essence evaporated into the void out beyond the light of every star, and when the Space Alien cavalry dropped him off on the world where they drop all aimless Abductees, he fell into a gutter for six weeks before a friend spotted him living like a vagabond and got him a job in construction. He worked that job honestly and hard for two months, and all that time he kept trying to find his sense, his purpose, anything but anything to give him a reason to live. But he couldn't find anything. He was still off balance and confused from the Space Pirates and the war and, and –

And.

III

Up until that time when he was twenty-eight years old, Walt Fulton had never been in love with anybody, not even the way kids let themselves moon at one another: it just never interested him, was all. He'd never so much as *been* with a woman. Or a man. Or even some Space Alien *thing.* It just never happened, was all. The Space Aliens abducted him when he was eight (or maybe nine, depending how you look at it), which meant that the only human people he grew up around were Abductees, and Abductees – everybody knows about Abductees. Abductees are *weirdoes.* Walt had the same impulses all guys do, but he was smart enough to shy away from Abductee women. It isn't good, getting involved with unstable people, and Walt knew it instinctively, even though no one ever explained it to him.

Knew it in spite of the way a couple times people tried to convince him that it wasn't like that. You know how that is – when somebody wants someone else, and they try to make them think it's all good and right and fine, and sleep with me baby it'll be good you know it's right, and like that. Walt was a pretty boy; times were he got it from all sides. But he never did, even though it tempted him. Even though there were times he was sure he wanted to, and times when he meant to go looking for that kind of attention.

When it came to it some part of him always eased away. He didn't understand why that was, and sometimes he even regretted what he never did. But he knew enough to trust an aversion that came to him so naturally.

IV

Some of the Space Aliens were okay, Walt thought. If they were regular people he might even be . . . interested in them. But they weren't regular people. At all. They were aliens – *Space* Aliens. And even if he thought they were okay guys and good friends, he never got an impulse to do *that* with a Space Alien. Maybe he could have learned to if he really tried. Maybe not. The idea didn't appeal to him.

V

The worst part about the fact that Walt Fulton never got *with* anybody was the way it didn't spare him the consequences.

He found out about it just before the War against the World, on the Space Alien flagship, when the Captain called Walt to his Sanctum and introduced him to his daughter.

A daughter, for God's sake! He'd never loved *anyone* before, and in the middle of his days he looked up to learn he had a little girl he'd never known.

A little girl nearly old enough to be a woman.

Walt still had nightmares about that meeting. He didn't like to think about it – times were he didn't even know *what* to think about it.

But he sure knew what he felt.

He hurt. He wanted to break down and cry every damn time he thought about that day.

And the Captain.

And the war.

And the little girl, and her *mother.*

And maybe that was a part of it, on the hill, in the

construction site: maybe a part of the reason he fell in love was because of what happened worlds away in space and time.

Maybe that was a lot of it.

He was the father of a beautiful little girl somewhere trapped a thousand light-years ago on Earth, and he didn't even know the meaning of love.

Until he met Lena.

There on that alien world thick with the teaming thousands the Space Aliens abducted between 1965 and 1980, Walt Fulton, lost in time and place and context, found a thing he didn't understand and couldn't ignore or deny. He didn't want it, but he didn't have a choice about it, either.

VI

Lena was more like a woman than she was like a man. She was *alien,* but not very alien. Even in that first moment when Walt saw her as she looked up as she walked past the construction site, he knew she was alien but thought of her the way he thought about human women.

That was a mistake. A really, really bad mistake. He didn't learn how bad it was till later.

She looked up as she walked by the construction site, and as she passed the breeze seemed to grow still.

Walt stared at her. She saw him.

And suddenly there was something in the air, an impossible something made from fine, complex chemicals – alien pheromones and stranger things. And stranger still the pheromones reacted, interacted, bound and bounded against one another until –

Until.

Walt felt his breathing stop, felt himself begin to spin –

She was beautiful.

She was wonderfully alien, more like a woman than

a woman is like a man. Her skin was pale, pale blue – not alien at all because a human woman's skin looks just like that if you watch her walking through the twilight.

She smelled like tarragon.

Before he even thought about it Walt found himself wandering away from the construction site.

It should have bothered him to do that.

He'd signed a contract when he took the job, and the man who'd hired him knew Walt Fulton was the famous Star Pilot and adventurer, the man who'd terrorized the Space Pirates till they'd hid where no light shines. And that man who'd hired him, he'd looked Walt in the eye and said *Walt Fulton, you ain't going to be here three weeks from now if I give you this job.* And Walt said *No, no, I take the job, I take the job, you can count on me.*

And he'd meant it, too. He needed to work and to sweat and to turn his mind away from the universe so he could *think*, because the battle at the War against the World bothered him, bothered him now and bothered him then, and not just because it was a battle but because that was where he met his little girl and that was where he'd left her, and now no matter how he tried he couldn't get back in through time to rescue her.

That bothered him a lot. He really really needed to think about it.

And he said *I take the job,* and he meant it, and now he made himself a liar on top of everything else.

But it wasn't like he had much choice. Something in the back of his brain came over him, took hold of him and dragged him away from the picks and shovels and the big earth-mover with its Space Alien engine. And all he could do was move. He dropped his shovel when it caught in the fence-gate at the edge of the site, and he kept walking until he could touch her – touch her cheek, caress it, gently, carefully, probing the alien texture of her smooth blue skin. . . .

He expected her to pull away from his touch, but she didn't. She stood still as a statue, watching him. Taking him in. She didn't speak or move; just stared into his eyes.

She could see deep down into him, Walt thought. He wasn't sure why he thought that, and he never learned whether or not he was right.

Then she kissed him, and Walt lost track of everything – where he was, who she was, what she was, all of it. Everything but the way her lips tasted like just-ground spice, and the way they pressed against one another, and –

She paused for breath.

And took his hand.

And led him away.

"We have to hurry," she said. "We have only a week."

Her voice was eager, excited. Frightened. It fascinated Walt, but he didn't understand what she was saying.

"A week. . . ?"

"I'm – metamorphosing. Changing from what I always was into what I'll always be. And when I'm changed I won't abide you."

Walt still didn't understand. He felt – he felt like she'd hurt his feelings, somehow, but he wasn't sure how she could have done that. "But why. . . ?"

"You won't abide me, either, Walter Fulton. She shrugged. "Why do you breathe?"

Walt laughed. "I have to breathe," he said. "That's how I get air." And laughed again when he heard himself, because he could see a way that made no sense at all.

"You can take me now," she said. "In a week that won't be possible."

Walt wanted to scoff. He wanted to say, *Oh that's so silly how can you say it?* He was confusing lust with love, of course. He almost understood that. But does it matter, really? Love and lust are sometimes two intimately related parts of a single process. God Made us as we are for good and sufficient reason, and our ignorance of the processes that consume us must surely be as deliberate a part of that same plan. *If I love you now I'll always love you, I wouldn't stop loving you just because you've changed what a silly thing to say, don't you trust me?* He wanted to say all those things and a thousand others, but he held his tongue. Because a part of him already knew what was going to happen. He knew, and the knowledge spoke to him, and he heard it. He could have stopped himself then and there – turned around, gone back to his work, and never thought of her again.

He could have stopped – but he didn't.

There were days when he regretted that. And others when he knew he'd done the only thing he could.

VII

She led him to a grubby apartment at the edge of the Space Alien quarter of the city, where they sat and talked and thought and stared at one another uncomfortably for the longest time. She served him coffee and oranges, and Walt wondered why she'd have earth-human delicacies like that in her cupboard, but he didn't ask.

"I was in the war," Walt said. "I fought with Space Pirates in their hideout beyond the light of the farthest star, and I lost. And they killed me, and ate me alive. When they were done they tossed my bones into the vacuum cold as the primordial absence of light."

He didn't know why he told her so much. He didn't like to talk about himself. Usually he tried to avoid saying who he was. Not that it helped, everybody knew.

"I know who you are," she said. "I looked for you. I'm glad I've found you."

Walt wasn't sure what that meant, but he didn't like the sound of it.

Not at all.

"Tell me your name," he said. "I should know who

you are, shouldn't I?"

She shrugged. "Lenore," she said. "Call me Lena."

That was a lie. He knew it was a lie. He wasn't sure how or why he knew, but he did.

"I've got a little girl," he said.

He didn't mean to say that. He never told anybody about his little girl.

She looked at him – quizzically? Was that what her expression meant? She looked at him out of the corner of her eye, and she said, "Go on."

"I only met her once," he said. "It was during the War against the World. I didn't even know about her up till then – someone stole my DNA –"

"Stole?"

Walt shrugged. "I don't know how. I never gave her mother a sample of me. But she got it somehow; I saw the DNA test. Pandora is more my daughter than she is her mother's."

"You never saw her after the war?"

That was the part that made Walt want to cry. He felt like he had an obligation to his little girl, and he meant to make it good. But no matter how he tried it wasn't any use.

"I never meant to be her father. When I met her she was almost grown. I've got an obligation and no way I could ever make it good. And no matter how I try . . . We got separated in the war," he said. "I keep trying to get back to her, but it's never any use."

Lena took his hand, squeezed it. "You'll find her," she said. "I know you will."

And Walt began to cry. He didn't know why. It made him feel stupid, but he couldn't stop no matter how he tried.

Lena reached across the table, put her arms around him. Held him and rocked him back and forth, almost like he was a baby.

After a long time she let him go. And took his hand.

And led him to her room.

Walt wanted to hesitate. Maybe out of shyness, maybe because a part of him thought sleeping with an alien was wrong. Maybe . . . who knows, maybe he had some intuition that sleeping with her would seal a fate for him he didn't want to live.

But whatever the reasons were, he didn't have the heart for them. He hurt too much to fight her, and when she came to him he didn't resist.

VIII

When Walt Fulton was eight he died in a car accident, and they buried him in the ground where no one could see the progress of decay.

When he was nine – nine? Does a dead boy age? – when he was still eight a year later UFO Aliens came down from the sky and Abducted him.

First they made him alive again.

That wasn't any big deal for the Aliens. Everybody knows UFO Aliens have magic powers of a highly scientific nature; it only stands to reason that they can teach the dead to live.

The Aliens made him alive and they set him loose, and when he saw that the earth wasn't anyplace for a boy who used to be dead – when Walt lost heart and despaired of the world, the Aliens came to Abduct him. At first he couldn't stand them, but in the end he went with them willingly. Even before they resurrected him they knew he would – sooner or later. But there's no denying that they did what they could to hurry him toward them, by sabotaging every effort he made to make a new life for himself among the world.

Half a lifetime later he died again, outside a spaceship in the deep black back of space, in a place so far from the rest of creation that the first good light from the dawn of time has not yet shined upon it. Some say that in a billion years that place will see the first trace light of the first star God created. But others say that it will never happen, because the gravity mass of the universe is too great, and even light cannot escape it entirely. They say the light will back around to circle the far end of where it started before it shines to break the dark.

That terrible darkling place where no light may ever shine, that place a million-billion miles from Walt Fulton's earth and his life and his death – that was where Walt Fulton died the second time.

He died in the middle of an terrible war, when his ship fell through time to the worst place there is and cannibal Space Pirates found him lost and alone and defenseless.

Space Pirates are like that. They'll kill you if they can, and eat you if you're tasty.

IX

When they made love it wasn't explosive or incredible or intense. It wasn't even – wasn't even very good. But something in the act touched Walt where he lived.

It was like – he didn't know how to think about it. Part of him wanted to think he felt fulfilled, but that wasn't right. It sounded stupid when he thought the word *fulfilled.* And it wasn't satisfied, either, because it left him feeling restless and unsettled.

It feels like – a ritual. Like love is a ritual that binds us together. Whether we mean it to or not. Yes, that was it – that was exactly the thing he felt. But he wasn't sure if that was just him, or the way he felt about his lover, or whether love was like that for everybody. It felt like he suddenly knew a truth about love that no one had ever told him, but how could it be that kind of truth when there were so many people who loved different people every night?

How?

Were they unhappy, unwhole, unbindable people? Were they just different?

Then and there he didn't think he'd ever understand. Later the question began to seem unimportant.

X

It is true that before he met Lena, Walt never – not in all the time he grew up, not in all his adventures or the War against the World or the horrible tortures that the Space Pirates committed on him – never once in all of that was Walt Fulton *with* anybody.

But he sure thought about it a lot. Thought about the weirdo Abductee women who eyed him hungrily; thought about people he never met, but dreamed he knew; thought about playing doctor with Erica Skolner back on Earth, before he died and the Space Aliens found him in his grave.

Walt wouldn't ever forget about Erica. He thought about her all the time sometimes. Before the car hit him, before he came back to life, the summer before all that horrible stuff happened Erica Skolner found him in Tim Fischer's tree fort, and she kissed him.

Even as young as they both were back then, Erica Skolner really knew how to kiss. Walt felt electric just remembering sometimes.

XI

When they touched Lena pressed him hard and . . . wrong. He didn't do any better. He scratched her once, and other times she seemed to hurt in ways he could not understand.

He hated when she hurt like that. It made him feel like dirt.

After a long time Lena turned out the light and they went to sleep.

Or tried to. Walt didn't sleep much. Mostly he stared at the alien ceiling, wondering what the hell he'd gotten himself into. When he finally did drift off, he didn't sleep well at all – he kept waking up, looking around and trying to remember where the hell he was, how the hell he'd ended up in a place that looked so wrong.

Not good. Not good at all.

In the morning Lena brought a tray of coffee and cigarettes, and woke Walt rubbing gently on his shoulder.

Of all the things that happened that week, coffee and cigarettes in bed in that strange alien room, lazing against a pillow and smoking and sipping – when he thought about it later that was the part that made him most nostalgic.

Walt's cigarette was still burning when the phone rang.

Lena answered, and after a moment she said it was for him. That made no sense at all, because there was no reasonable way that anyone could know to find him here.

But he took the phone, and said hello, and it was Rick Mitchell at the other end of the line – and suddenly the call made a kind of sense.

Walt had known Rick Mitchell almost all his life. Rick had ways of knowing things about him that Walt couldn't begin to figure.

Rick sounded worried.

"You're okay," he said. "You left yesterday. No one saw you go."

Rick had helped him get the construction job. Rick had helped Walt a lot since they'd found one another on this world. Walt wasn't sure why the other man looked after him, though he was glad he did. Walt still wasn't himself, and he needed friends looking after him – he was still shook up and bothered inside, from the Space Pirates, from the war, from a lot of things.

But he didn't know what made Rick so eager to help him. It'd been so long since he'd known Rick – Walt tried to remember the last time he'd seen him, before they found each other here. Wasn't it that awful time in the schoolyard, with the other boys calling Walt things like Zom-boy and Dracula, and throwing dirt clods at him? After Walt died in the car accident, after the Space Aliens found him in his grave a year later and brought him back to life, in the middle of the week when he ran away from them and found his parents and tried to start his life where he'd left it when he'd died? Walt was pretty sure.

"Rick," Walt said. "It's good to hear from you. How

did you find me here?"

"It wasn't hard," Rick said. Which had to be a lie. "You'll come in today?"

"I . . ." Walt knew he wouldn't be back today, or tomorrow, or the next day. He wasn't sure he'd ever go back. It best to tell the truth, wasn't it? "I won't be in this week."

Rick didn't answer right away. "We'll expect you," he said. And then the line went dead.

What the hell was with him? What was he trying to do?

"What did your friend want?" Lena asked him.

Walt shrugged. "I'm not sure," he said. "I guess he wanted to make sure I'm all right."

"Are you?"

Walt laughed. "Of course I am." he said. "Aren't you?"

Lena didn't laugh at first, but that was okay – aliens never get it when you tell a joke, not till they have time to realize. When she laughed she smiled, and her smile made her beautiful.

"We ought to go do things together," Walt said. "Isn't that what lovers are supposed to do?"

Lena smiled again. "If you think so," she said, "then they are."

Walt laughed. "I want to show you . . ." he said, ". . . everything! But we haven't got the time."

She took his hand.

"Let's go," she said.

Walt rolled his eyes. "We can't go out yet," he said. "We aren't even dressed." He grabbed her smock from where she'd left it last night, on the back of one of the kitchen chairs. Tossed it to her.

Or did he toss it at her? He might as well have, the way it turned out. She didn't see it coming, didn't expect it, didn't even imagine that he might throw a shirt at her.

It hit her in the face.

That was bad. He knew the moment it hit her, knew from the moment she made that sound like a predatory bird about to strike –

Before he could ask her what was wrong she was all over him. Grabbing his collar, lifting him out of his seat, shaking him, raking his face open with her talons sharp as knives.

She nearly burst his eye. If he'd flinched, if he'd struggled, if he'd even had time to ask her what the hell she thought she was doing, just that much movement would have shaken her foreclaw off his eyebrow, where it'd caught, and into his eye.

So fast he didn't even feel it. He didn't feel anything at all – nothing but his own blood dripping on his collar bone.

After a moment she drew back in shock. She looked as if she only just realized what she'd done.

"I –" she said. And then she couldn't say anything.

Walt was afraid – he tried to tell himself he shouldn't be, that it was just an accident, a misunderstanding like you always get when two people so alien to one another spend time in the same room – but hard as he tried he couldn't make himself believe it. Not for a moment. He was scared out of his mind, and every moment that went by he became a little more frightened.

After a long moment she let go of his collar, and he eased away from her until he could feel a door against his back.

That was the bathroom door, wasn't it? All he had to do was slip into the bathroom, close the door behind him, and he'd be safe. She wouldn't be able to get through the door, would she? And even if she would, it'd take her a moment, and a moment was long enough for him to figure out how to run away. . . .

He went to the bathroom cabinet, looked into the mirror that hung above it. There was blood all over him. She'd given him a deep, ugly gash – so deep that he could see white hints of bone where she'd torn his forehead.

Walt swore.

He didn't like to see his bones.

Seeing his bones made him think of this grave back home, of the dark of space where no light shines, of pirates roasting him alive, eating him. . . .

. . . .his clean bones adrift and revolving in the blackness of space.

He'd seen enough of his bones already. He didn't ever want to see them again.

He opened the bathroom cabinet, fumbled through it, looking for the first-aid kit. Hoping against hope that Lena's biology was enough like his that they could use the same antiseptics –*yes,* there it was, a spray-can of bandage foam. He picked up the can, cocked it above his eye. Squinted and sprayed the foam into his wound. It bubbled down, turned to liquid slowly, and fed into the skin.

After a moment the bleeding stopped, and Walt began to wash the blood away.

Washing meant getting his whole bloody damn head into the sink, and when he did that he couldn't hear anything over the water from the tap. Which is why he didn't hear when Lena opened the door. He didn't hear her step into the room; he didn't see her walk across the room to stand beside him.

Didn't hear the way she sobbed when she saw him dripping wet with blood and water.

When he realized she was there it scared him half out of his skin. He saw her in the mirror and for an endless instant he knew he had to run for his life because she'd come to kill him, but there was nowhere to go but into the shower stall, and that wasn't anyplace to escape.

And froze in terror.

And stared at her through the mirror, terrified, waiting for her to murder him, trying to think how he could try to escape. But he couldn't think of anything.

So he kept waiting for her to kill him, but she never did. After a while he began to realize that she didn't want to hurt him after all.

Or maybe she just didn't want to hurt him any more than she already had.

She looked so sad, so helpless – it made him hurt to see her like that.

"I'm okay," he said. "Don't worry."

She stood beside him shivering. Sweating thick, oily blood-dark beads of perspiration.

She smelled like cumin.

She made that sound again – like a sob, but dry.

He wanted to hold her.

"It's okay," he said. "Everything's going to be okay." And he took her in his arms, and held her for the longest time.

"I'm sorry," she said. "I'm so sorry."

"Come on," he said. "Let's go. Get dressed."

As he followed her out of the bathroom, the smell like cumin changed to cardamom. In the air behind that was the steam from Turkish coffee.

XII

A river run beneath the universe and time; underneath causality that doesn't work the way it should there is a river made of timeless time.

Oh, it's not a place with water running down some continental trough; it's not a river that way. It's a place like a metaphor, and what runs through it isn't any material fluid but the current of our collective fate. The Space Pirates learned to sail this river half a billion years ago, and until Walt Fulton came onto the scene they used the advantages the river gave them to wreck havoc everywhere – lately and most notably on Space Alien starships.

Walt Fulton stopped them cold.

It wasn't hard for him: Walt was the Boy Who Came Back from the Dead. He'd already lived and died and lived again; he knew *The River of Our Destiny* instinctively no matter how he'd never sailed it. When Space Pirates dived out of the universe and deep into the river, they were safe from the Space Alien Navy. But they weren't safe from Walt. Walt always knew just where they'd rise back into space and time; he knew to go there and wait for just the moment when the curtain of reality would peel away to admit the Pirates.

Walt Fulton killed a lot of Space Pirates.

They hated him for that.

And when they had their chance they made him pay.

With all his heart and soul.

XIII

While they were getting dressed he said, "I want to take you to the beach. The beaches on this world are strange – wonderfully strange."

It was the wrong thing to do. What he should have done to save what little sanity he had was kiss her sweetly on the cheek and say he'd call (a lie, of course; the right thing was for him to never call again) and walk away as quickly and directly as he could without abandoning his dignity.

But it was a stupid thing to do for other reasons, too. Even if he wasn't going to walk away, he should have known better than to go strolling on the streets of the Alien Quarter, both of them with their beach towels and dressed in t-shirts and swim trunks. The Alien Quarter in that city on that world of Abductees isn't anyplace for a casual stroll, and even if it were it sure isn't anyplace to walk around dressed down half-naked for the beach.

Alien People stared at them – gawked and snickered and made jokes just out of hearing. Even the streets seemed hostile – but those streets always seem to spite the human understanding. They don't divide symmetrically the way we know all roads must – they split and resplit to form a lunatic paisleyesque pattern men and women cannot navigate, no matter how long they endure them. Even with his map – Walt always had his map with him when he traveled through the Alien Quarter – even with his map in hand Walt could hardly find his way.

Just outside the Alien Quarter's central square (which is not square at all) Walt stopped to check his map. Stopped too long, the way it happened: for when he looked up to ask Lena a question, she was nowhere to be seen.

"Lena?" he called. *"Lena!"*

But there was no answer. He looked back and forth and back again, trying to find his lover in the Alien grotesquerie that was the strange unbeautiful unsquare alien square, but he could not find her.

XIV

For the longest moment after he lost Lena, Walt Fulton contemplated going home to his apartment and crawling into his bed with its cool smooth sheets. Forgetting Lena, and what they'd done together. Forgetting where he was and who he was, and trying to pretend he was still a little boy back home on Earth.

He could pretend the Buick had never run him over, that he'd never died, that the Space Aliens had never resurrected him to fly out across the stars and have adventures and get eaten by Space Pirates.

That was maybe the most important thing about Walt: He never got to finish being a boy, and because he never did all his life he wanted to go back and pick up where he'd left off. But of course he never could.

He knew that. There were days where he had to make himself remember or he'd just sit down on a bench someplace and stare at the horizon forever.

Which wouldn't be good. It'd be stupid, too. Walt had a reputation as a hero ever since his first fights with the Space Pirates, back when he was still a boy. But there were lots of days when he wondered what people were thinking of when they said he was a hero.

It's never good to curl up and deny the universe around us, not even for people who are busted up inside, the way Walt Fulton was.

But running away, in that moment and that circumstance, from the horrors that and already trapped him forever and always into a fate he never meant to find – that would have been a better thing than what he did.

We live and learn. And some of us, like Walt, can learn by dying, too.

XV

Walt spent ten minutes staring at the xenotic crowd in the Alien Square, trying to spot Lena, before it occurred to him that she'd gone on without him. That had to be the thing: she hadn't noticed when he'd stopped, and kept going toward the beach? She probably didn't even realize they'd become separated. He had to keep going, wait for her there at the beach. She'd show up sooner or later.

So he took another long hard look at his map, found his bearings, and made his way to the dune-ridge that separated the beach from the Alien Quarter. When he got there he stood atop the ridge the ridge for most of an hour, watching the empty beach and the streets that led to it. Watching and waiting and just knowing that he'd catch sight of Lena any moment now, she head to be coming, didn't she?

But she never did, no matter how long he waited.

After a while Walt fell asleep on that unearthly dune beneath the cool blue Alien sun.

When he woke he saw that his map had got caught in the breeze and blown away.

XVI

Remember this: the Aliens resurrected and Abducted Walt despite the fact that there are an easy hundred thousand living folks upon the Earth who'd give their eye teeth for five good minutes of Abduction.

Walt never forgot it. Not for a moment.

But he never understood it, either. How could he? Aliens are hardly ever sensible. It's no mean feat to comprehend them.

Even for an Abductee.

Oh, once when he was older somebody told him that they took a dead boy because it'd make a hole in the world if they took anyone alive, and there were too many millions of holes already, everything had grown unstable.

And that was true enough.

But the greater truth is that UFO Aliens don't hesitate to make a hole in the world when they get a mind to, no matter what the consequences. Even the earthbound can figure that, just listening to the stories the Abductees bring back.

The real reason the Aliens took him was because Walt

was Walt and special in his own way. Especially for a dead boy. Even among the Aliens – who are special by definition because every last one is different from the all others entirely and absolutely.

XVII

When he woke three hours later Walt Fulton decided it was time to head back toward the square, hoping Lena would be waiting for him there. He couldn't find his map, but he was sure he knew the way.

Which was a foolish notion, surely.

For somewhere along the way he made a wrong turn and ended up in a part of the Alien Quarter even more alien than all the rest – a place where the street signs were written in a script Walt had never seen and could not hope to read.

He kept going, because sooner or later these streets had to give way to something he recognized, or something with English street signs, at least.

But they never did. Maybe he'd got himself stuck walking around and around in circles; maybe this part of town was just too complicated to walk away from without guidance.

Late in the afternoon, he rounded an obtuse corner and came upon a straight and narrow humanesque street, a block and a half of apparent sanity in the midst of the alien chaos. It would have been a godsend if it had been alive and thriving. But it wasn't. All the shops on both sides of that street were bricked up and abandoned.

All of them but one.

The open shop had a great plate-glass window, and in the window there were neon signs:

SOLVE
All the Mysteries
of Life

• • •

Love
Health • Happiness • Business
Past Lives • Fortune
The Interpretation of Dreams
The Reunion of the Separated

And, cut into a grey steel plaque in the lower right corner of the window:

Miss Samantha
Palmistry, Tarot Readings
Astrological Charts
Visions Through the Crystal Ball
Fully Guaranteed
ONE VISIT WILL CONVINCE YOU

On a card that hung from the door knob:

Readings
$5.00
Tuesdays and Thursdays
Noon to Six

Walt peered into the open door beside the window, but there wasn't much to see – it was dark inside that place, and probably abandoned. He leaned into the doorway, called into the darkness: "Hello. . . ?" he said.

There was no answer.

There's no one in, that's all, he thought. Or maybe "Miss Samantha" was in the back, or upstairs, or, who knew what, but there had to be a Miss Samantha or the shop would be as much a ruin as every other on that block.

Didn't there?

And the shop had have the sort of phone a human man could use, didn't it? If Walt could find a phone he could call a cab to take him from that awful place.

So he pushed into the damp dark empty anteroom, and through the door of beads at the far end of it. That took him to an even-darker room – a peculiar room with fake stone walls and a fortune-telling table set with half a dozen chairs.

There was a glowing crystal sphere on the table.

Somewhere back behind him the street-door slammed shut of its own accord.

"What the hell?"

There was a placard at the near end of the table, a folded strip of card stock with two words printed on it. He could just barely read them by the glow that came from the crystal:

WALTER FULTON

Words came to him from no place he could name: *Sit down.*

"Who?" Walt looked all around the room, trying to find the source of the voice, but he found nothing. "What?"

Someone had known he would be here.

Someone left this place waiting for him.

Space Pirates.

Some kind of an ambush – he'd fallen into a trap.

Space Pirate traps are always like that: they find a place in space and time where you're tired and alone, and fall on you while you're off your feed, damn Space Pirates always the same, he hated them sometimes.

Time to get out of here, he thought, and it was true, he did have to get out of that place or the trap would spring around him, damn Space Pirate trap you can never guess which way it's going to open, but the plain truth was that Walt Fulton was tired and grouchy from wandering all day among the aimless streets, and he wasn't in the mood to walk away from a fight, if they wanted him they could come and get him damn the Space Pirates anyway he'd face them on their own terms.

That was what he thought.

And it was right, so far as it went.

But he didn't even guess the nature of the trap that sprang around him, because he'd lived it all his life, and would live it far into his future.

So he sat at the chair that waited for him, against all common sense and judgment, and waited for the trap to make itself apparent.

A moment after he took his seat the air around the crystal began to crackle with static electricity, and an image grew inside the glass — a red, fibrous, pulsing image that grew larger and larger until it seemed to fill the sphere.

Walt recognized the thing inside the sphere. He recognized it by the fine patina of scar tissue that mottled the bloody fleshy surface, recognized the shape and texture of the scar, that was the scar that covered his own heart. He'd seen it before in the worst possible circumstances, and he could feel deep inside him beating out the rhythm in the crystal ball.

The hearts of resurrected humans always bear similar scars. There's a peculiar but unimportant flaw in the resurrection process that scars each of them distinctively.

When the image in the sphere reached the limit of the glass, Walt felt the pressure in his chest, and he knew the trap was on him in a way he hadn't figured, and he was dead, screwed, gone, lost in the Alien Quarter on a planet in the middle of nowhere with no goddamn cavalry anywhere to find him oh shit bastards no damn damn damn.

XVIII

As the room went dim around him Walt Fulton closed his eyes to die, and when he did he had the strangest vision. No life-before-his-eyes vision this time, no matter how he'd seen that twice before: this time he saw Lena staring at him through his dying dream, and his little girl beside her, calling to him, terrified.

That was strange enough, but it wasn't the worst of it by far.

The worst part came as he saw the two together, and noticed a likeness that he'd never found before.

XIX

This is what a geas is:

Walt Fulton only met his daughter once. He met her when she was fourteen on a spaceship in the middle of a war, and before the moment he set eyes on her he didn't know he was a father.

Walt Fulton hardly knew his little girl Pandora. And even so he knew he had to find her; to save her; to do every single thing he could for her.

He was her father, after all.

XX

As Walt Fulton slumped lifeless on the table, his head came down against the crystal sphere, pushing it from its setting on the table. The sphere rolled for a long slow moment before it reached the table's edge.

And then it plummeted to the floor, only half a moment before Walt Fulton could let his final breath.

When it struck the floor, it shattered, and the spell that meant to kill Walt Fulton was broken.

Or maybe it was only freed to find him and to plague him all his days. Spells do such things, you know.

Walt woke a moment later, dizzy and weak, to see a hot green mist rising from the shards. As he watched the sphere released its final telling, a telling Walt would have avoided if he'd known what he was seeing.

But he didn't know, not at first.

At first it was just a picture, the image of the wrecked field outside Cincinnati, Ohio, in the middle of the War against the World.

He recognized that moment, that place, that time – no, he didn't recognize it, he'd never seen this moment, this was the moment perpetually denied to him, this was what he'd never seen, the light, the red light everywhere, and look how the great Space Alien battleship – *Walt's* ship – dropped to the ground to crumpled like an aluminum can under the tire of a truck.

And now a figure emerged from the wreckage, oh dear Lord my God his daughter his little girl Pandora running from the wreckage of the fallen battleship and out across the battlefield with guns blazing and rockets blasting and rays burning in every direction.

He screamed at her, he shouted, *Pandora, Pandora, you're going to get hit get cover hide get out of the line of fire they're going to kill you, girl, don't let them kill you,* he shouted and shouted at her but there was no way that she could hear.

Till now she stumbled too close to a bright red fire.

A time fire, Walt thought. That was exactly what he saw in the vision: a blazing burning mass of time gone mad, trapped at the southeast corner of the battlefield that was the War against the World. *That's why I can't get back to rescue her – that time fire locks everything for days and parsecs.*

The time fire flickered and flared in the far corner of the battlefield as Pandora ran toward it.

And as she drew near a bolt of red lightning shot out at her just the way ordinary lightning draws to ground. Pandora was a lightning rod for time, and the fire was time searching for ground, and when the bolt struck her she vanished as though she'd never been there.

She's fallen out of time, Walt thought. *I'll never find her.*

And then he saw her reappear – on the far side of the battlefield. She looked awful. *Awful.* Blood all over her, and a look on her face like she hated herself worse than the weirdo Abductees hate themselves. – That wasn't her blood, was it? She wasn't broken or wounded, and she'd have to be torn to shreds to bleed that much. What happened to her when she fell out of time? Why did she hate herself so much?

Then suddenly the vision grew distorted, as though time were warped and broken just a moment ahead – as though waves of calamity were roiling backward from the future.

And in the distortion Walt lost sight of Pandora. He saw a watery-bright smear as something bright and hot shot down at her – a missile? A burning fragment of debris, and that was the end of her.

And then the distortion brightened and intensified, till now everything on the battlefield turned to light and fire as the world exploded.

As the vision of the broken glass caught fire and exploded, and everything around Walt turned to light.

XXI

There are dreams that Spacefarers get sometimes. Prescient dreams? It's hard to say. They spend their lives immersed within the river of time (known more formally as *The River of Our Destiny)* that runs beneath creation, and after a while the current finds its way inside them, and whispers dark and dreadful things to them – things that no one ever ought to hear.

Some times it speaks to them in dreams, to tell them of their fate; but other times it only lies to them, offering visions to possibilities made of irony and dread.

The blast that tore the tarot-house asunder was partly made of light and fire, but it was partly made of time, too. When it engulfed Walt Fulton the fire burned him and the blast broke him, but before either of those things could take their toll the time-blast tore him from the moorings of his *here* and *now,* and sent him drifting on *The River of Our Destiny.*

He drifted there in agony for a time that never ended, aching, burning, wishing he could die and never dying; floating on the substance that is not time or space but stands in stead for them in that place beneath the moorings of the universe.

The river gave Walt Fulton visions as he floated on it. Some of them were lies and some of them were honest portents, but all of them were torment made to break his soul.

XXII

In that place where there is neither time nor place there is a vision of Walt Fulton as an old, old man, caught in time and shackled to obligations too terrible too deny and too forbidding to obey. He is in the bridge of a peculiar spaceship, and there is a girl with him. The girl is at once human and alien; too mundane and otherworldly.

The girl is his daughter. Her name is Pandora.

"This is where it began," Walt Fulton hears the old man he may and may not become say, "on a godforsaken isle in the deep black back of space." The old man seems to marvel at the possibility as he turns his pitch-empty star-globe over and over in his hands.

The little girl leans closer, struggling to hear the old man's quiet voice.

"I was alone and away from everything and everyone I ever knew," he says. "I was lost to time and forever – stranded a billion light-years from the first light of creation."

The little girl takes a long moment to digest this. "I don't understand," she says at last. "Why wasn't there any light? Why couldn't you see the stars?"

The old man frowns.

"The universe is an enormous place," he says. "It hasn't found its own ends yet." He pauses. "There are those who say that it makes them, extends them every moment – that as the first light of the moment of creation reaches out, it extends ahead of it the far edge of the universe. And every day it grows larger and larger ahead of the wake of light. . . . but that doesn't matter. Not so that you or I could tell it. Because there are ten million light years between the edge of light and the far bound where distance simply ceases to be. And when my ship blasted itself through time, it sent me out into the depth that makes that void."

XXIII

Watching from his dying and undying perch upon the river, Walt Fulton of his *here*less and *now*less present wondered at the significance of the vision. Was this an honest telling? Did the vision mean that there was a way for him to find his daughter? And if it did, would it leave him old and haggard, bent by time?

Or was this only an irony, the sort of irony that grows so naturally in *The River of Our Destiny*?

Some ways, they say, universe is made of irony. Ironies like that one are there to tempt us from the purpose of our lives until we windmills all our days.

XXIV

There's something strange about the way the girl and the old man interact with one another. It's like – like there's something between them. Affection? Love? It could be either one of those. But – they don't seem to know one another very well. Look, look at the puzzled expression on the old man's face when she speaks to him – as though he weren't sure how to take what she says to him.

As though she didn't yet know how to wrap him tidily around her finger.

"Daddy," Pandora says, and hear how awkwardly the word trips across her tongue, as though she were uncomfortable using it, "why did they kill you? Why were they Pirates? Why did they eat you alive?"

The old man blinks and blinks – as though he can't imagine how to answer questions that don't admit his assumptions.

Perhaps he can't. But he tries.

"Pirates always kill people when they find them," he says. "It's just the way they are."

Pandora frowns. "I know lots of people," the little

girl says. "I know bad people too. I met a lady who killed a baby once. And she was *bad* bad, too." Pandora stops a moment. Thinks about what she's saying. "But everything they do there's a reason behind it, and the reason – it's part of who they are."

The old man frowns.

"You know what I mean?"

He nods.

"Then tell me what makes them into Pirates."

"It's the wrong question," he says. "Space Pirates aren't regular people turned crazy enough to kill. Well, maybe some of them. But not most! Most of them – it's like they're born that way. Like all the awfulest people everywhere in the universe are drawn away and turned to Pirates. Really! – Don't look at me that way. I know Space Pirates. I was with them and they killed me. They ate me alive. . . ."

The old man trails off. He's thinking, thinking – trying to figure out how to say what he knows he has to tell his daughter. Trying to turn what his heart knows into words and reason to share with someone else, only he has to say it gently because she's just a girl, after all, just his baby girl even though she's been through hell and all the world collapsing around her.

But the trouble is that when he looks at it, when he thinks about it, the ideas fall apart on him.

Because the truth is that she's right: even Space Pirates have reasons for being who they are. Space Pirates have hearts and minds and motives; in their own strange way they have nightmares that govern their behavior just as our dreams guide us.

XXV

The vision of the old man and the girl *was* a lie. Fate was being cruel to him, tempting him with a vision he could never turn to anything alive, and the only thing that he could do was close his eyes and blind himself to it.

But he could not close his eyes. He watched the vision despite himself, fixated, unable to relent.

XXVI

The old man who is or will be or could be or won't be Walt stops himself.

Pandora is a little girl. How can he tell her – really *tell* her – what happened when the pirates killed him? How can he tell her what he saw inside the hearts of the Space Pirates as they butchered and ate him? Walt Fulton who's been dead and alive and dead alive in his day knows all too well that the dead are aware of their surroundings, even if they care very little about them. Even if the pain and the panic and the passion left him with his last breath, he still knew the world around him. Even when that world was no world at all but the black pit of lightless space. And he knew the Space Pirates as they butchered him in the vacuum, and knew them intimately as they gorged themselves on his steaming bleeding flesh.

Walt Fulton *knows* Space Pirates. There are none who know them better.

"But why?" asks his daughter who three days ago he hardly knew. "How are there so many born so mean? How do they all know to become Space Pirates?"

And maybe, Walt Fulton thinks, maybe there just aren't any answers to her questions. Maybe a little girl Space Alien who spent all her days on earth and knows her world by the rules of character and motivation – maybe a little girl like Pandora just can't understand about Space Pirates born to hate and hunger out beyond the last light of God's creation.

And maybe that's for the best.

Walt Fulton really truly tries to believe this. He does not have the heart to believe anything else.

He doesn't have it in him to tell her the truth – it's as simple as that.

"Their mothers choose them specially to be so cruel," the old man says. "They wouldn't have it any other way." But the truth is that he doesn't really know the answer to the question. He fought them lots of times, especially back when he was just a boy Abducted into the Space Alien Navy. But until the year that he turned twenty-eight he never really *knew* a Space Pirate. And when he knew her he loved her.

He only loved her for a while. And afterward he was so sorry that he couldn't say.

XXVII

No!

Walt Fulton couldn't stand the thought he saw painted on the old man's face. There was a wistfulness there, a longing for a thing Walt knew and denied, a thing that he could never bear and could not abide. He writhed against the *here*less and *now*less ether of the river underneath all worlds, trying to reach through time to grab the old man by the collar and demand to know what the hell he thinks he was thinking of – and as he did a current caught him, dragging him away from the vision of the old man and the girl.

For a long momentless moment *The River of Our Destiny* became a blur of time gone bad that appeared to Walt Fulton as a grey-red haze – the mélange of all his days and years, and the days of others, too. And then the moment cleared to reveal the place and time from which he'd fallen in the Alien Quarter of the nameless Abductees city. He saw Lena walking the streets quickly, purposely, as if she were hurrying toward an appointment.

Look how she walks, Walt thought. *She understands those*

streets.

That was impossible, of course. Those streets were mad, mindless – beyond the capacity of any mind to comprehend.

Weren't they?

She's an Alien.

The words unsettled Walt in a way they shouldn't have. He knew she was an Alien, and he'd known it from the moment he'd set eyes no her.

Hadn't he?

Or had he? And it came to him that he hadn't really known until that moment, not in his heart. Not until he saw her understand a thing no human could comprehend had it come to him that

that

"Lena?" he asked. His voice was a harsh throaty whisper, the shadow of a voice – something had broken in the blast, and it wasn't getting any better as he floated in untime. "Lena, what *are* you?"

And Lena turned to look him in the eye, right through time and space and possibility, she saw him there no matter how she never could, she saw him and she said, "Walt Fulton, I'm the one who loves you. What else would you know?"

And Walt felt every burnt and blasted hair on his body try to stand on end, and he reeled back, trying to find his sense of the order of the world –

And Lena disappeared. The whole vision disappeared, in fact.

XXVIII

Walt Fulton reels back, back, all the way back into his past until he reaches a loop and gets snagged in it.

He hates that loop. He's hated the memory of it ever since it happened, and he hates it now as it recurs before him: that awful moment in the Captain's Sanctum, just before the War against the World.

He watches himself storm out of the Captain's Sanctum, heading toward the docking bays, where he takes a scout ship and dives into the blackest part of space.

Watches himself sail among the stars for most of half an hour, subjective, trying to clear his head.

It was a pretty damned inconsiderate thing to do to the daughter he'd only just met. He knew it even then, but he'd needed time to think, to cope, to try to come to terms with the circumstance that found him.

When his head is clear he drops the scout back out of space to face his little girl and the War against the World impending.

And everything goes wrong.

One moment Walt Fulton is booming back into that here and now above the battlefield in southwestern

Ohio, about to rejoin the battle to destroy the world. (Yes, destroy the world. Fulton is a Lieutenant in the Space Alien Navy; he and his cohorts have literally set out to clean all life from the surface of the Earth. The ways of the Space Alien Navy are strange, impenetrable, and not very nice.)

Walt Fulton sees the Space Alien fighters crowding the sky; sees the Earthling jets scattered and burning as they plummet one by one to the ground; winces at the sight of so many of those he might once have loved dying so brutally. He doesn't want this battle, and he doesn't like it, but he is a boy who takes his blood-oath to the Space Alien Navy very seriously; if the battle before him is a the War against the World where he was born, well, that is his war and he'll see it through.

Or so he tells himself.

And then suddenly something is wrong. So very, very wrong. There's a flash of red that stretches out to the horizon and up into the stars, and suddenly Walt Fulton is falling through space time and causality to the farthest place beyond the stars.

Falling through the nature of the universe. Falling crosscurrent against the physical laws that bound his atoms into one another, and if it weren't for the acausal improbability reflectors in his fighter scout's engine his chemistry would have forgot itself.

He would've atomized.

Someone watches him as he falls. He can feel it. That sounds strange, you'd think, wouldn't you? How could someone see him falling crosscurrent against the nature of the universe? Falling so far across the temper of creation that when he finally comes to a halt he is out beyond the farthest light of the original creation – how could anyone, *anyone,* see such a thing in progress? But those questions misunderstand the nature of the universe. There in the probabilistic underbelly where the thread of our destiny flows like a river below cause to guide the events that shape our daily lives, distance and vision are a matter of perspective.

Of course they are.

There on the river of all destiny everyone is plain to see for what she is, what he is, and Walt Fulton is no exception: everyone who sees him pass knows who he is, where he's been, where he's going. Wouldn't you? – Walt would have known those things about the watchers, too, if he hadn't been too stunned and distracted to realize that they were there.

But he doesn't even think to look up as he falls across the universe and destiny.

Bad mistake. Bad bad bad.

For while that ungodly place holds no attraction for decent ordinary folks, it's a keeno hideout for Space Pirates. And if he'd had enough sense to look up as he fell Walt Fulton would have seen them watching him.

Falling.

Falling and falling beyond destiny the universe and fate, until he reached the place where no light shines.

XXIX

The Space Pirates have a great laugh at Walt Fulton's expense. They think it's just the thing to see, watching the hero of the spaceways tumble head over heels across the universe and destiny. But at first it doesn't matter. Walt Fulton the falling hero doesn't even see them making fun of him, and he never has cared much one way or the other what Space Pirates said about him behind his back.

The trouble is that they watch him, good and hard, the whole damned way he falls. And it isn't lost on them where he ends up.

XXX

When he finally comes to a rest in real (albeit virgin) space, it takes Walt a good minute and a half to figure out where he's ended up.

Five minutes after that to chart a course through space and time back to Earth and the first moments of the War against the World.

And three long hours of relativistic eternity (a thousand years of untime passed around him, but Walt never felt it) to come back to life time above the battle –

And something goes wrong.

Again.

Even wronger than it went before.

Last time when he tried to come to time above the battle he'd managed at least to get there for a moment of it. But now all he sees is red, red everywhere bright to the horizon swallowing the stars, and then he falls back across the river that runs beneath the universe.

XXXI

Seven times Walt Fulton tries to join the battle that he never should have left, and seven times he falls out of destiny to come aground beyond the fist light of creation in that place so far beyond the center of creation that the first light of the big bang won't reach there for a million years.

And six times the Space Pirates watch him, and they laugh uproariously and the broken hero destroying himself a little at a time trying to insert himself in a time and place that will not abide his presence.

It takes them six times to realize that they have Walt Fulton at their mercy.

That's another thing about cannibal Space Pirates: they aren't always any too quick on the uptake. Lots of them are pretty damn stupid, in fact. What do you expect, after all? Smart, well adjusted people to go around robbing and butchering Space Aliens? I don't think so.

But then there are those who make all sorts of excuses for the little darlings. Your mileage may vary.

XXXII

When the Space Pirates find him in the place where no light shines, they break his ship in their trap they crack it open they pull him out much the way a hungry man will pull a lobster from its shell.

When they have him, they shot him. Four times. They do not shoot to kill him; that would have been a kindness, in its way, and there is no kindness in these Space Pirates.

Instead they maim him.

A blaster burn down the center of his spine – not deep enough to paralyze him, much less relieve him of the pain they will inflict on him. It is a very careful burn that sets every nerve inside of Walt on fire and leaves them all blazing for as long as he lives.

Which is not long.

The second blast unmans him.

The third turns his left arm into a shriveled blackened relic, cauterized where the embers meet his shoulder.

The fourth tries to do the same thing to his right arm, but something goes wrong. Where the blast should leave a neatly cauterized crispling husk, the burn-seal ruptures, and a wide artery sends Walt Fulton's blood spasming out across the void where no light shines. As it flies it crystallizes in the infinite cold, till now it scatters like sand across the hull of the pirates' station.

XXXIII

Walt Fulton, floating on the ether of the river of his doom, closed his eyes. He couldn't stand the sight before him. He couldn't live with the memory, and couldn't bear to see it alive in person happening all over again, it was going to drive him out of his mind he closed his eyes.

That spared him nothing. In his mind's eye he saw the beautiful lady Space Pirate, tearing a hunk of him off his dying body – eating him alive.

No no no please God no I don't want to see it.

But it was no use. He opened his eyes again, to see –

To see.

Two things he had not see that awful moment as the Space Pirates ate him alive.

The faces of the Space Pirates.

Two of them.

The near one, the beautiful woman drawing his severed arm through the anti-osmotic screen that is the visor of her helmet.

And the one behind her.

Her commander.

XXXIV

The woman is Lena.

The commander is Walt Fulton himself – wild-eyed and unshaven, looking like a drunkard.

XXXV

Walt Fulton screams just as the cavalry comes over the hill and to save him. In a moment the Space Pirates will break and run, and the cavalry will reassembled the disparate bits of his corpse and drew his essence back into its mortal coil. When that's done they will debrief him, and find him shell-shocked, unfit for duty. In due course they will take him to a world where they think he will recover.

They will think that world is right for him. The people who live there are like him, after all. They are earthling Abductees, most of them people the Space Aliens took from the world between 1965 and 1980. And that's Walt, isn't it? Walt is an earthling Abductee, and those are his core years – the ones he lived in most of all.

But those people aren't his people. Nothing about them could make a home for him.

Instead of healing him, the world the Space Alien Navy takes him to will disquiet Walt. It will shake him until he is a mumbling wreck, and then it will give him love.

XXXVI

After a long while *The River of Our Destiny* grows still, and Walt Fulton begins to wonder if he will spend the rest of all eternity in this state, watching the worst bits of his life loop past him, again and again and again. He'd rather be dead, he thinks, really dead, dead so dead that the Space Aliens can't find you and make you live again, damn them anyway.

Not that he really has a choice, and besides, if the Space Aliens are damned there isn't a whole lot anybody can do about it anyway.

XXXVII

After a timeless time that seems to stretch forever (and maybe it *does* stretch forever – time is like that on *The River of Our Destiny)* the emptiness grows bright again, and now he sees the old man and the girl again, there on the space ship.

The girl *(Pandora,* her name is Pandora, and she's his daughter, damn it, not some girl) the girl Pandora looks at the empty globe.

Frowns. Looks up at old man who is her father in this undream.

"We have to go there, Daddy," she says. "You can't leave a thing like that behind and never face it."

The old man Walt Fulton looks like he wants to cry.

Like the whole idea terrifies him.

Scares him out of his mind.

Of course it scares him out of his mind!

"Every damned time I think about that place," he says, "I see that image. The woman I loved carving out a pound of me, searing it with her blaster, and eating me alive –"

The girl Pandora frowns. "Space Pirates," she says.

The old man swears. “I don’t want to think about Space Pirates,” he says.

But it’s all over his face: he knows the girl is right.

And Walt in the ether knew it, too: he had to go back to that terrible time and place and confront them.

How could he ever be whole until he faced them?

And of course the answer was that he never could.

XXXVIII

Walt closed his eyes again.

He thought about the vision of his dismemberment in the place where no light shines.

The faces.

It was a lie, he thought. *That wasn't me, and it wasn't Lena, either.*

Later he will learn that he is wrong.

XXXIX

Walt Fulton opens his eyes again and for half a moment he's watching the old man and the girl again. They on the ship, plunging through *The River of Our Destiny,* and Pandora points into the void that hangs above them. "There, Daddy, *there.*" The place she points is black as pitch, and deathly cold; Walt who watches knows it in his heart, no matter how he's never yet set eyes upon it.

The old man takes the helm of his ship, and drops his ship out of the unsubstance of the river –

And just as the vision of their destination congeals before them, a pale blue-green hand reaches into the *here*less and *now*less river to take Walt Fulton by the collar and heave him back into his *here* and *now.*

For half a moment he saw Lena standing above him in the wreckage of what not long ago was Miss Samantha's parlor.

"Walt. . . ?" she said, he heard her say. But he did not answer, because he could not answer, his throat is a bloody wreck of torn flesh and pulped cartilage, and there in the real world where time consumed it it grew worse by the instant – *"Walt!"*

He swallowed hard but carefully, trying to clear the blood welling and leaking through his throat. "Let me go," he whispered. "It's time."

Lena shook her head.

"No," she said. "I won't."

Walt Fulton blinked, slow and careful because his eyes ached and burned, oh God oh God he hurt so bad it hurt to blink. He said, "I love you, Lena," and he didn't know why and till that moment all he knew was that he felt bound to her and drawn to her and he didn't know what love was but he would have said no that isn't love, I'm not in love, if this is love there isn't any point. But when he said it he knew that he meant it, and he knew it was real and as important as anything he'd ever lived.

She said, "I love you too," and he believed it when she said it. But he didn't know why, no how, no way.

And then the injuries consumed him, and Walt Fulton died.

XL

And Lena put her arms around Walt's cold, still body.

And lifted it.

And carried it away.

XLI

Walt woke in an ancient spaceship, strapped to a resurrection machine that looked as though it were even older. The ship was so primitive that Walt had never seen anything like it before in all his days – so ancient that it took him a long moment to realize that it *was* a spaceship.

If it weren't for the navigation holo near the forward end of the cabin, Walt might never have known where he was.

The resurrector was easier to recognize. Walt knew all about resurrectors, as far as there was anything to know. He remembered how the aliens used one to pull him out of his grave when he was a dead boy, and the cavalry had to use one on him when the Space Pirates killed him.

Resurrectors are always the same. The same panels, the same shape, the same controls and diodes. Sometimes Walt thought they'd always been just like the ones he knew, forever and ever, back to the beginning of time. Maybe they had been, too; no Space Alien Walt ever met remembered where they came from. No one he knew understood the machine's design or structure, nor the details of its form and function. Once he heard that the resurrectors dated from an intergalactic civilization so far in the past that no one remembered them anymore.

Maybe that was so. Or maybe the Aliens who designed them came from the far side of the universe. Who could say? Who could know? The bigness of the universe goes on forever, and sometimes the most important things get lost in the endlessness of detail.

Lena stood beside the resurrection slab, operating the machine.

"You died," she said.

Walt didn't understand. "What do you mean?" he asked.

Lena frowned. "Your heart stopped and your brain died and when it was gone your essence faded toward oblivion." That sounded so silly, the way she said it. So solemn, so serious. Walt wanted to laugh. But it wouldn't have been nice, and anyhow she wasn't being silly. You could measure things like that with the dials on a resurrection machine. Back home on Earth what she said would have been crazy-sounding and theological, but when a Space Alien said something like that she meant it, plain and simple. "I carried you to the spaceport north of town – my ship is here."

Walt rubbed his eyes. He was trying to remember, something, trying to remember a nightmare. . . .

"I didn't know where else to find a machine," Lena said. "I had to hurry. Whatever touched you touched you hard. It drew your life away. Very quickly."

"I don't remember," Walt said. But that wasn't complete true, because the nightmare was coming back to him already, bits and pieces as disjointed as time upon the river.

Lena looked at him steadily. She didn't say a word.

"What was wrong?" Walt asked, nodding toward the readout arm on the resurrector. "What did it say?"

Lena shrugged. "An explosion," she said. "Material and temporal blast. I had to pull you from the River."

Walt wanted to pretend he didn't know the River that she meant, but he knew too damned well, he remembered a lot of things now, he remembered, remembered –

Remembered.

"I saw you, Lena," he said. "You did something to me, and I never thought you could."

Lena winced. "The River lies sometimes," she said. "Don't believe everything you see."

Walt frowned. Nodded.

Looked around the cabin uncomfortably.

It was a strange, strange ship, unlike any ship Walt had ever seen – and oddly familiar, too. What shipyard would build a ship like this? He imagined a shipbuilder a million years ago, on a planet that no longer had a sun – that was the feel of this place, Walt thought. It was a tiny bit of a world that no longer existed.

"Where did you get this ship?" he asked.

"It's been in my family forever," Lena told him. "Do you like it?"

Walt smiled. "It's beautiful," he said. "I love it."

XLII

She took him to the bridge, where they looked out across the spaceport through the ship's wide glass bay. The port was like every other spaceport Walt had ever seen: crowded and ugly, like a parking lot back home on Earth. Crowded and ugly as a junkyard – almost every ship Walt could see was a battered old junker a million years older than time. Walt was amazed that scrap-heaps like those could lift themselves off the planet, much less sail across the stars and time.

He scanned the horizon, strained his eyes until he saw the city – south of them, almost farther than he could see from here. Three miles away? More? It was hard to judge distance across the glassy brightness of the plain.

East of them, on Walt's left, he could see the ocean.

"There's something else I have to show you," Lena said. "Something that you need to see."

She led him away from the bridge, down a long corridor that bent again and again until he lost all sense of where he was and where he'd been. She stopped in a place where the hallway narrowed between two doors. One of those was and ordinary spaceship door, light *fabriqué* that wasn't quite enough to give you privacy, even though it meant to be; but any door that could really close a room would be more drag than anyone wanted to haul across the stars. . . .

The other door was different. It was a security door, and the moment Walt saw it he had to know what hid behind it. Lena tried to warn him about that door. She put her hand on his shoulder and said no, Walt, you don't want to do that trust me no you don't, but Walt didn't listen. He knew better. Of course he did!

If there was anything in the universe Walt Fulton had to know, it was the mystery on the other side of a locked door.

He didn't know why; if his life had depended on it he couldn't have given a reason.

But he knew he had to.

It was like – like the door was a secret fear he'd always hidden in his heart, always known but never met. And the moment that he saw it he knew he had to confront it.

He pressed his palm against the lock plate and the door's outer panel clacked free of its catch. It shouldn't have. Palming the lock shouldn't have done anything unless Lena had scanned his palm-print into the ship's log.

It was like – like the ship already knew who he was, without any introduction. Like it always knew who he was, even if that was impossible.

Walt pulled away the security door and saw there was another door inside it, an airlock door made of heavy die-cast metal. The metal looked like iron, but it probably wasn't – Space Aliens hardly ever use iron for the things they build. Walt wasn't sure why.

Now Lena touched his hand. "Don't open that, Walt," she said. "It's dangerous." But it was too late when she said it; Walt already had the latch all but disengaged. Besides, Walt already knew. Of *course* he knew it was dangerous. Everything about that door screamed *Danger! Danger Will Robinson!* Something in him drew him toward the danger anyhow. Maybe he was suicidal down inside so deep he didn't know about it, or maybe there was something in the danger that he had to know no matter what. Who could tell? The unconscious mind is like that, sometimes. It draws us to do the damnedest things we never thought we'd try.

It was dark inside the airlock. Dark as night.

Walt leaned through the door to look into the dark. He felt a static charge as he did – it felt as though he'd passed through an anti-osmotic field. In just a moment he knew that was exactly what he'd done.

Because the place the airlock led wasn't in at all, but *out;* when Walt's head passed through the anti-osmotic field he heard vacuum space scream against his eardrums; and everywhere around him there were stars shining clear and small and round, brilliant as only stars in raw cold space can shine. High above him a great red sun consumed half of the apparent sky.

As soon as he heard the scream in his ears and felt the void against his skin, he pulled away – but his shoulder caught against the airlock, and before he could free himself the light and the vacuum and the stars scalded his face.

Lena stood touching-close behind him.

"I nearly fell into a sun," Walt said.

"Be careful," she said. "The ship doesn't always know when to stop you."

Walt's ears rang; his eyes stung. He could feel a sunburn all over his face like he'd sat out on the beach for weeks without a sun screen. "I don't understand," Walt said. "It's like all of space inside that thing." And then the obvious occurred to him: if outside was black space around a red giant sun, Lena had carried him away from a world he hadn't meant to leave. "Where are we, Lena? Why did we go?"

Lena laughed. "Silly boy," she said – said it indulgently, fondly, like it was something she loved instead of something to condescended to – "Silly boy, we didn't leave anyplace. My ship is in the spaceport yard north of the same city you woke up in this morning. I carried you here when you died, but I never carried you away."

She was holding his hand. Walt couldn't remember when she'd clasped it – just then it felt like she'd always held his hand. But that wasn't so, and it wasn't even possible.

"I don't understand," he said. "I looked out there. We're in orbit around a hot red sun. It's as big as the sky."

Lena rolled her eyes. "We're aren't there," she said. "This is a special ship. There are space distorters built into it – if you looked outside you'd say it's bigger on the inside than it seems from out there. Many times bigger."

Walt didn't know anything about space distorters. He'd never seen anything like that – not in all the years since the Aliens took him up to space.

But then he'd never been in a ship like this before, either – never even heard of ships like this.

"What does that have to do with the red sun outside that door? How can that be there if we didn't go anyplace?"

"It's the center of the distortion," Lena said. "It's the door into forever."

" 'Forever?' "

"That's what my mother always called it. It never goes the same place twice."

Walt stepped back from the airlock, leaned against the wall behind him. *Door into forever? Distortion?* He'd never heard of either of those things. And he'd never heard of doors that led across space so you could stick your head out into the shadow of a sun.

"I don't understand," Walt said. "How can that be? – if there were things like that around Space Aliens would use them instead of spaceships. They'd be all over the place."

Lena rolled her eyes.

"It isn't like that," she said. "It doesn't go where you want like a spaceship does. It goes where it goes." She shrugged. "There isn't any way you can understand it, looking at that door."

Nobody had to tell Walt what nonsense was when he heard it. He shifted on his feet, leaned back against the wall opposite the airlock. "Who made that thi – ?"

And suddenly the wall collapsed behind him.

And he fell into a room that he'd never seen before but always carried in his heart.

"The door is a worm-hole," Lena said. Walt hardly heard her. "But that isn't any use all by itself – it never goes anyplace you want, no matter what. The important part isn't the door, or the worm hole, but the river. If you open a wormhole at relativistic speed, the ship falls into Underspace."

Walt hadn't ever heard anybody say *Underspace* before, but he knew all about it. Most of the most horrible things that ever happened to him happened on account of a relativistic wormhole and Underspace and the horrible Space Pirates who lurk there.

But Walt wasn't even paying attention. All he saw was the inside of the room.

And the window.

No way he could have avoided seeing that window – it would have been hard to avoid seeing it. Spaceship windows have to be small and strong to stand against the night-hard vacuum of space. Almost every spaceship window ever made is small and round, like a porthole on an ocean liner. But not this window. It was big and broad like the window in Walt's bedroom back home before he died, and it had nice blue curtains, just the same. Nice but not too pretty, curtains like you'd see in a boy's room – homey and rough and just exactly right.

Walt knew those curtains. He could never have forgotten them. He knew the whole damn room the moment he set eyes on it. Of course he did! This was a place just like the place inside him, the place he always carried in his heart even though he'd left his mother's house when he was eight.

Three big framed photos on the walls – pictures of the football team he played on the year that he turned seven.

Walt was confused. Why was his room here? His room back home on Earth in his mom's house? – No, he thought, this wasn't his room. It couldn't be. It was a duplicate, a counterfeit someone made to fool him –

"Why?" he asked. "This isn't my room. Why did you make it here?"

Lena shrugged.

"It's real," she said. "It was always here for you; it always will be, so long as you live. This is the room in your heart."

Walt sighed. Why so much double-talk? Why wouldn't she be straight with him?

"How did you know? Why did you make it?"

Lena shrugged. "I never did," she said. "I couldn't. This room is yours."

Walt was by the window, now. For a moment he hesitated: he was afraid to part the curtains.

Afraid of what he'd see when he did.

Because he knew exactly what he'd see.

Before he looked. Before he so much as touched the curtains. He'd've known it with his eyes closed, it was that fundamental to his heart.

It really was. He knew so certainly and with such

conviction that his own sureness scared him worst of all.

Because he was certain, and he was right.

And when he parted the rough-and-pretty curtains he saw exactly what he knew he would: his own grave, open and inviting, just the way it'd been the day he'd crawled away from it.

XLIII

Walt kind of lost it while he was looking at his grave. He started crying big heavy sobs that made him shake all over, and he collapsed into his bed that was exactly right when he was eight but now it was too small by far. Lena came over and held him, and that was nice, but it wasn't right because she wasn't mom and mom didn't love him anyway, mom gave him to the Space Aliens because she couldn't cope and he ran away and fell bear shit in the woods and the Space Aliens had to save him, and he hated that, hated that so much it made him cry so bad, no matter how life worked out pretty good all in all, no matter what went right, no matter how he was the hero of the spaceways scourge of the Space Pirates, Walt Fulton missed his mommy because she didn't love him.

mommy mommy mommy I love you mommy please take me back mommy I love you mommy

but mommy never would.

Mommy wasn't like that. She got all hard inside

when he was dead, and when he came back to her she never could accept him.

Last year during the reconnoiter before the War against the World, Walt went back home to her, went home to see mom and dad and his sister and all his friends even Tim Fischer, and when he got home mom was dead. Gone. Died when he was twelve, the way things turned out. But Walt was the Boy Who Came Back from the Dead, and he knew how to talk to corpses in the ground because once you've been there you can't ever forget. So he went to his mother's grave, and he told her he loved her, and missed her, but no matter what he said she just ignored him. He talked and talked to her until Old Man Fischer called to him.

Old Man Fischer's grave was almost always empty, on account of how the old man had gone on to his reward, but when he heard Walt Fulton calling to his dead mother he came to see what was the matter.

Let her be, Walt, the old man said. *It isn't right to taunt her.*

He startled Walt. "I never did," Walt said. "I wouldn't. I love my mother."

I know you do. But she never did recover, Walt. She never learned to love you after you returned.

Mommy howled down in her grave when she heard that. Walt wanted to comfort her, but there wasn't any way.

"I love you, Mom," Walt said. "You know I always will."

She did her best to ignore him.

She knows, Walt. She knows. Some day she'll love you, too.

XLIV

When Walt finally stopped crying Lena took his hand and led him away to show the rest of the ship. It was a marvelous ship, an incredible ship, and if he'd only thought awhile he'd've realized why it seemed at once so strangely *alien* and at the same time so familiar.

That ship wasn't like any ship he'd ever stowed aboard; it was nothing like the fighters he'd commanded in his battles against the Space Pirates and the rebel dynasty and the world at home. But he'd seen ships like this a thousand thousand times. Never from the inside, though he'd seen the insides of ships like this floating ruined wrecked and laser blasted in the dark among the stars.

Because that ship was a pirate ship.

The product of ten billion years of separate and discrete Space Pirate tradition passed mother to son, father to daughter across the endless span of time and space and fluid causality along *The River of Our Destiny.* He'd wrecked a thousand ships like this. If anyone had ever told him that his secret heart was a tiny room in the center of a pirate ship, Walt would have laughed at them.

Destiny is like that. Walt Fulton knew best of all.

But he didn't connect what he knew to what he saw, didn't even recognize the walls around him.

He might've if he'd looked back as Lena led him out of the ship onto the glassy rocket-blasted plain that was the spaceport. If he'd looked back as they walked south toward the city he'd've seen the ship from the outside, and there's no way he could have failed to realize exactly what that it was.

But he never did.

XLV

The main road from the spaceport to the city ran along the sea, but Walt and Lena didn't use it on their way back to the nameless city of the Abductees. They were too far inland – almost as far from the water as they were from town. So they wandered south through the spaceport, south and around past a thousand ships, junkers and jalopies and things so strange it was hard to tell whether they were old or new or fallen out of time.

Somewhere along the way the spaceport metamorphosed into a junkyard. Walt never noticed the transition. He just looked up and noticed that the ship in front of him wasn't a ship at all but a shattered, blasted hulk, and when he looked around he saw that all these ships were just as moribund.

They came to a barbed-wire fence just beyond the far edge of the glassy plain, in a place where a chalk-cliff hung over a junkyard. Walt liked barbed wire. It made him think of home – of the barbed-wire fence at the edge of the highway way out past Old Man Fischer's place.

Walt gathered the coils of wire carefully together, pulled the fence aside as though it were a curtain.

"Step through while I hold this open," he said.

Something skittered somewhere close to him, and Walt saw sparkling green light in the corner of his eye. He looked down just in time to see a hairless alien rat scurrying for shelter. Hairless? Maybe it wasn't hairless. There were shards of emerald embedded in its skin. They glittered like crystal hair in the sunlight as the creature burrowed into a trash heap.

"It's nothing," Lena said. "They hardly ever bite."

Walt shuddered. He didn't want to think about what a thing like that could do to him – he really, really hated rats. Especially when he thought about the rats that found him in his coffin.

He was still shuddering when he began to follow Lena around the cliff-base, kept shuddering as he followed her along the narrow paths that led through the great mounds of debris.

Shuddered again when they rounded a corner and saw four chittering hives of alien rats, nests so dense they seemed to pulse and writhe against the surrounding debris.

"I hate rats," Walt said. "I really hate them." But he couldn't bring himself to tell her why.

Where they'd started the junk all looked ancient, as though it'd been rusting in that yard for a million years – maybe more. As they moved south the wrecks seemed to grow younger and younger, till now there were Earth-cars in the rubble – mostly old fish-finned Chevys from the sixties. (Walt wasn't sure why, but almost all the Earth cars here were sixties cars. Maybe someone had Abducted a trainload of the things, or maybe people made them to look that way because they missed cars the way they were back home when they were young, or something. He wasn't sure.) And now suddenly the junkyard changed again, and the wrecks weren't car wrecks but spaceship wrecks, Space Pirate ships blasted and torn to bits – and look, there, up there on the high summit of a mountain of shattered fighter cubs – the Space Pirate base.

Walt would have known it anywhere.

He couldn't ever forget it. The dusty crystal blood scattered on its hull; the blast-marks he'd cut into its hull in the moment that the ship had dropped out of time to find him, just before it broke his space-scout –

It was the ship the Space used to captured him out beyond the first light of creation. They took him in there, and they cooked him alive, and they ate him.

There was an image Walt could never forget: that Space Station, out in the distance, and in the foreground a green-skin Space Pirate woman chewing on a hank of him she'd cut away with her blaster, flashed cooked with its beam. She lifted his pound of flesh to her mouth and tore a bite of him away with her teeth, and she laughed and laughed but there was no way to hear her in the absent void of space.

Walt could never forget that Space Pirate woman. He thought about her all the time.

Thought about her as he climbed the mountain of debris. When he saw the image of her green Space-Pirate face in his mind's eye, there was something – something familiar about it. Something he needed to realize but couldn't bring himself to see, kept trying to figure out what it was all the time he spent climbing up the mound. It didn't do any good; he couldn't put it together.

And then he was at the crest of the pile, touching the broken station. Wiping his finger across the hull.

His finger wiped across a fine patina of brown grains.

Grains of his own blood scattered across the spaceship's broken hull like powder-brown primordial dust.

It was the ship that killed him. There couldn't be

any question.

How could the broken ship be here, on the same world he'd ended up on himself? Why would the Space Alien Navy bring it here to junk? Why would they even bother hauling it away from the far void beyond the stars? It wasn't like it could be hazard to navigation a million light-years beyond the far edge of the universe.

Unless they hadn't moved it.

Unless somebody else moved it. But who? The Space Pirates? That was silly. Space Pirates don't go around cleaning up their messes; that isn't their way. Tidiness is as alien to them as, as. . . .

As alien as they are.

Alien Aliens, ha ha ha ha, Walt thought. And he laughed inside his head.

And laughed and laughed.

XLVI

There was a diner on the far side of the junkyard, and since Lena was tired they stopped at the diner for coffee.

There wasn't anything strange about that. Not a single thing.

Not until the pay phone in the back by the bathroom started ringing.

It was a clunky painted-iron coin-op phone, the kind of pay phone you would have seen in a diner in Chicago in the fifties. Until it started ringing Walt thought it was strictly a decoration.

A pay phone. Wired into the Space Alien comm. net.

There were stranger things than that on worlds like this – not a lot of them, but more than a few. Walt had seen a bunch of them not an hour before. But no matter how strange the phone was, it was nowhere near as strange as what happen when the fry-cook answered it.

"You want to talk to *who?*" the fry-cook said. "What

do you think this is, the Space Alien Navy? – All right, all right. I'll ask." He cradled the phone against his shoulder. Looked around the diner with a rueful expression on his face. "Walt Fulton," he shouted, "telephone for Walter Fulton. Is Walt Fulton here?"

Walt swore. "Who the hell?" But the fry-cook was too amazed to answer. He just held out the phone, waiting for Walt to answer the call.

It was Rick Mitchell on the other end of the line.

"Rick," Walt said. "How did you find me here?"

Rick ignored the question.

"You're all right," he said. It wasn't a question. It was like that with Rick ever since Walt had run into him on this world: he always spoke in patterns Walt couldn't unravel. Sometimes Walt thought that was because the world back home had changed between the times they were Abducted; other times he was sure it was just Rick acting like a nut.

"I'm fine," Walt said. "Don't worry."

Rick took three long moments to respond. "I'm . . . worried?"

"Really, I'm okay," Walt said. Too quickly.

Rick's tone made him uneasy.

"When I was little –" Rick said, "– old man Fischer. You remember old man Fischer? Tim Fischer's grandpa?"

Walt knew things about old man Fischer he couldn't ever tell anyone.

"When I was a kid old man Fischer taught me this . . . trick. It's, like – when you clean a chicken, I mean. In the guts. He showed me how to read the future out of chicken guts."

He waited for Walt to say something. Did he expect Walt to be derisive? That was silly. Walt had seen stranger things than people looking for the future in the entrails of poultry.

"What did you see?"

"Something bad. It's going to happen to you. I saw

your face, and then it twisted, and . . . I don't know what will happen."

"I don't want to know," Walt said. He found himself relieved that Rick Mitchell couldn't tell him anything else. "I know what's going to happen. Don't tell me anything more."

Rick didn't answer right away, and when he did he sounded terrified. "Next week?"

"Next week."

XLVII

They left the diner just a few minutes after Walt got off the phone. They kind of had to leave; the whole damn diner was staring at them, and there was nothing left to talk about, and after that call Walt couldn't think of anything else anyhow.

A few blocks from the diner the road toward the city crossed a freeway. It was tricky walking there – there were sidewalks, but they were badly marked, and the traffic came up and down the ramps too damn fast. Drivers didn't pay any attention at all.

That was where it happened, the awful business with the truck.

They were passing through the nested ramps and access roads, and Lena was out ahead of him crossing the deltalike junction where the second ramp bled out onto the street.

Walt called to her. "Wait up," he said. "You're getting ahead of me."

And she turned to answer him, right there in the

middle of the lane. "What –"

That was all she said before the truck splattered her across the pavement.

Her body mushed, tumbled, bounced on the truck's fender like a sack of broken toys. And fell against the curb a few inches from Walt's feet. The truck didn't even slow down; it screeched around the corner and sped south toward the city.

That moment always stayed with Walt as long as he lived. The way the air smelled so thick and full and rich, like windstorm blowing open a spice house – tarragon, nutmeg, cinnamon, thyme, other smells like oranges or cheddar, maybe bitter iron, he wasn't sure.

He knew she was dead and wouldn't answer any questions, but he tried to talk to her anyway.

"Lena – ?"

He crouched to look at her, hoping against hope that her eyes would open, that she'd answer him, that she'd be all right and everything would work out the way he always dreamed it would, but he knew better. He could see how she looked, and it wasn't good. Not good at all. The truck hadn't broken anything off – most of her body was still attached to her torso – but lots of her had scraped away. On the fender, the pavement, the curb.

Oozing down onto the sidewalk.

Walt couldn't think. He couldn't imagine what he ought to do. All he could do was crouch beside her, dumbfounded, staring at the person he thought he loved or cared about or something, the person he never meant to attach himself to but attached him anyway, the woman he loved who wasn't any woman and he didn't even know if he loved her, damn it, and now she was purple-red meat and bone and cartilage pounded tender on the asphalt in front of him. Whatever he felt about her he felt it still, now and forever and always.

He ought to call an ambulance, he thought. Somebody with a resurrection machine. Or pick her up and carry her back to her ship where she could save herself, where he could put her in the resurrector and revive her. But he didn't do that. He did the damnedest, stupidest thing, and even though it worked out in the end he never got over how stupid and ugly and dumb and perverted he was to do it.

He bent down, pulled her body up off the curb.

And kissed her lips.

He put his hand beneath her neck, forced his tongue into her mouth, forced air into her lungs. He tried desperately to blow the life back into the raw warm meat that was her body.

Disgusting. Absolutely disgusting.

He hated himself for it at the same damn time he did it. He tried to stop himself, but he couldn't. Something deep deep down compelled him, and no matter how ashamed he felt, no matter how he dishonored the dead and ignored all sense and decency, he couldn't stop.

Couldn't.

Not even when his lips and mouth and throat got tinny with her purple blood.

Not even when he felt his gut lurch and heave dry spasms that wanted to turn into something worse, but he couldn't dare, no matter what.

No matter what.

He didn't stop the resuscitation when the world went grey around him because he wasn't getting enough air for himself. The grey didn't last long: after a moment it turned to black, and Walt blacked out just long enough to lose his balance.

When he picked himself up off the curb he saw that Lena had begun to breathe without him.

XLVIII

Walt took Lena's wrist, felt for her pulse. He found it – throbbing gently, all but imperceptibly. He leaned back, looked at her. She'd changed, he thought. Her wounds had dried and crusted; a grey congealing mass covered the places where the asphalt had ripped her skin away down to the meat.

Walt let the hand that held her wrist slide down to hold her hand.

And he watched her.

And watched her.

Watched her barely moving, staring amazed and agape as her body pulled itself back from the dead before his very eyes. As her flesh writhed and twisted, frayed ends of torn muscle, bone, and tendon seeking each other out, knitting themselves back together.

Her skin rippled and pulsed as it stretched to cover her crusty dry muscles exposed to the air. Strange things bulged and quivered among the alien organs in the softness of her abdomen.

As bit by bit by bit her body pulled itself whole.

When most of the crusty scabs and pussy coagulations had dried and flaked away, Lena opened her eyes. She looked at Walt, and for a moment she looked relieved. "Home," she said.

It looked like it hurt her to speak.

He lifted her as gently as he could.

And carried her away.

He took her home to her apartment, the grubby worn-down place in the Alien Quarter where they'd spent the night before. Carried her into her bedroom, tucked her between the sheets, and curled up beside her.

IL

Lena woke in the middle of the night. Her skin felt cold and wet, slick with oily sweat. She smelled like cardamom.

"This isn't home," she said. "You didn't take me home."

Walt bit his lip. "This is your apartment," he said. "You took me here before."

Lena shook her head.

"This isn't home," she said. "It couldn't be. Home is my starship."

"Is that important? Do you need me to take you there?"

"Not now. Not yet."

L

She didn't wake again that night. Didn't so much as stir until late in the morning. Walt held her all night long. Rocking her, humming to her sometimes. He fell asleep around midnight, but he never let her go. When he woke in the morning his arms were still wrapped around her, protecting her, soothing her. He could feel her pulse against his wrist, feel her breath sifting through his hair.

I love her, he thought. *I really really do.* But he wasn't sure what love was, except love like he felt for his mom and his dad and his sister, and even though that word was the same Walt had a feeling that it wasn't the same love at all, just something related the way snow is kind of like ice is kind of like slush. *I love her love her love her.*

But he didn't understand how, and he knew it.

He was so afraid she'd die again. So afraid. He was afraid even though she was getting better – he had to be afraid. He couldn't bear to lose her. Not again. Not after she died, after mommy died, after he lost his little girl. He couldn't stand to lose anybody else. But that was part of loving anybody, wasn't it? People live and die and fade away, sometimes they run away and sometimes they change. Anybody you love you got to lose sooner or later, don't you? Walt knew that. But it didn't help. It just made him want to run away in a spaceship, go out into the black alone with nobody he loved and nobody he knew, and look for some Space Pirates to kill.

He owed the Space Pirates a death or two, too. It was a fair debt: They were going to get theirs. Sooner or later, probably both.

He looked down at Lena. Looked down at her face. Her skin was different now. Before it was pale and bluish; now it was different. Green, almost.

Space Pirate green.

She nearly looked like a Space Pirate, Walt thought.

A lot like a Space Pirate.

An awful damn lot like a Space Pirate.

Walt untangled himself, rolled out of bed. Went to Lena's kitchen and rummaged around until he found something that looked like it might be coffee.

When he came back she was sitting up, awake.

"Walt. . . !" she said, "I've missed you!"

Walt blew steam off the top of his coffee cup. Behind the nutty musky coffee smell there was citrus peel and clove. That was her, wasn't it? Or was there something strange brewed into the coffee?

"I've been dreaming –" she said. And then she hesitated. "– it seems like centuries. . . ! I know it's been only hours. This happened to me once before. When I was younger." She looked down at her claws. They were greener than her skin. "I'm metamorphosing," she said. "Too soon."

Walt felt his stomach lurch. "You're changing?" He didn't want to hear it. Didn't want to *know* it. "What will you become?"

Lena looked up at him. Shook her head. "When I was twelve," she said, "I fell onto a train track. The wheels cut me in three. I was lucky someone had the sense to shove the parts together, or I'd have imbecile sisters. . . ! Not really, of course. But a doppelgänger that doesn't start out with at least a bit of brain doesn't know much. It takes them years before they begin to remember who you are."

"I don't understand," Walt said. "Do you mean you won't remember?"

"No. I just won't care. That's all."

Walt couldn't imagine that.

"People always care," he said. "Sometimes they don't admit it to themselves."

Lena's eyes glazed; her face went slack. For three long minutes it looked like she just wasn't there inside herself.

"How come you didn't die?" Walt asked. "How come you don't need a resurrector?"

Lena shrugged. "It's my family," she said. "We've always been this way."

Walt turned away, took a long drink of his coffee. It was still warm. "Sometimes I think that most of life is trying not to think about dying."

Lena's eyes closed. Her ears twitched. "I never think that way," she said. "It makes me feel so bad." When he listened to her voice and pretended not to hear the words, it sounded to Walt like she didn't understand the problem. She sounded honest; she sounded shocked; she sounded sincere. But she didn't sound like anyone who'd ever lost someone she loved.

"There's nothing to do about it," he said. "You learn to live with it." But that was a lie. Walt never learned to live with being dead and losing people who he loved. He never got used to it. People live with death or they don't; they don't have any other choices.

Lena didn't answer. After a while Walt set his coffee on the nightstand, crawled into bed, and curled around her. He didn't sleep – he couldn't, not with the coffee

– but eventually she seemed to. She fell asleep after a while, and her dreams were nightmares. Walt could tell. It wasn't hard to tell; she writhed in her sleep, sweated a thin, clear oil that smelled like lime.

He watched her face as she lay sleeping. The gentle curve of her nostril that sloped in a concave arc out from her cheek puffed and puffed with her breathing. Her eyebrows twitched erratically, irregularly. Her skin grew greener and more waxy as the sweaty oil beaded up through her pores.

Then he saw that her eyes were open.

"What were you dreaming?"

Walt watched her blink three times. Her eyes dilated. Her pupils were horizontal slits, like a horse's.

She shook her head. "About you. About things happening to you." She reached over to the nightstand, took his coffee, drank some. Walt thought it had to be cold by now, but she didn't seem to mind. "We've only got a few hours left. The accident hurried my metabolism. The metamorphosis is almost finished."

Walt nodded. "Yeah, I thought that. I saw you change."

"I won't see you again . . . afterward." The muscles of her face contorted, and he thought that the light reflected in her eyes seemed very, very sad. But maybe he imagined that.

The phone began to ring. Lena went to answer, but Walt stopped her. He knew who it was. He knew what it was about. And he didn't want to hear it – not a single, solitary word.

LI

After a while Lena started to moan.

Walt didn't like that. The sound was haunting, terrifying. It made him feel afraid.

"Can I help you?" he asked. "Tell me what I can do."

But she didn't answer. She just moaned, and moaned, and now and then she panted. She was like – like the woman Abductee who went into labor a few weeks after the Space Aliens Abducted Walt. Just like that, Walt thought – panting and hooting and trying to control her pain until she couldn't fight it anymore, and then she began to moan. Once she shrieked so long and so high and so hideous that the sound left Walt shivering.

The tremor lasted five long minutes. No matter how he tried he couldn't stop it.

LII

Lena was still moaning when someone started pounding on the door.

It's the neighbors, Walt thought. *They're tired of the noise.* But what could he do about it? It wasn't like he could tell Lena to shut up and suffer quietly.

Screw 'em.

He ignored the pounding. Took Lena's hand, squeezed it softly. He bent to kiss her cheek, but stopped when he saw the tissue there was strained with marks like scars, blistering welts that looked about to rupture.

He kissed her forehead instead.

His lips came away from her slick with the pungent oil that covered her skin. Walt tried not to taste it. He wiped his mouth on his left sleeve, but that didn't help – it just spread the oil around, and the flavor was all over the inside of his mouth, bitter and sharp, burning like acid or worse, and he wanted to spit and Lena hurt too bad to notice but he still couldn't bring himself to spit away her kiss where she could see, he held his tongue and swallowed and his head swam there was something in that oil like a drug he felt so dizzy.

And the asshole neighbors were still pounding on the door.

"Go away!" Walt shouted. But of course they didn't listen; they only pounded harder, harder, till now it sounded like they were trying to break down the door.

I need to call the police, he thought. But there wasn't time, because the door was buckling and any moment it would give way, and now Lena began to scream, and there was no way he could step away from her when she sounded like she was about to die. . . .

That was when he realized.

What he already knew. About the change.

That was when he realized what Lena was changing into.

"We need to go back to my ship," she said, panting. "I need the resuscitator."

As the door broke open.

As the phone rang.

As Rick Mitchell stepped trough the broken door, gasping for breath.

LIII

For almost the first time since he'd woke to this world, Walt Fulton really *looked* at his friend Rick Mitchell. Noticed all the little odd things about him, like the way Rick was ten years older than Walt, even though they'd been boys together. That wasn't all that strange; Walt was a Space Pilot, and Space Pilots wander back and forth through time all their lives. It's only natural that they fall out of sync with their closest acquaintances.

But there were strange things about Rick Mitchell that weren't natural at all.

The scars on his face, for instance.

Till that moment Walt had seen them as complexion scars – ordinary acne scars. Lots of people have them. Lots of people have them worse than Rick Mitchell did. But now Walt could see they were the mirror of the welts rising on Lena's face, and he knew there had to be a connection between Rick and Lena.

A connection Walt didn't even want to think about.

"We've got to get out of here," Rick said. "Something really awful is about to happen."

And suddenly Walt was afraid.

More frightened than he'd ever been dueling with Space Pirates or fighting in the war.

"What?" he asked. The phone was still ringing, ringing ever since Rick broke through the door. He ignored it. "What do you mean? What do you know?"

Rick shook his head. "There isn't time to tell you," he said. "We've got to go."

Walt didn't like it. There was something wrong. Bad wrong. He didn't know what the hell it was, but he knew he couldn't trust it.

Trust him.

Trust Rick.

"You heard me," Rick said. "Come *on.*"

No.

Walt shook his head. He stood up, blocked the way between Rick and Lena.

"We aren't going anywhere," he said, "until I know what's going on."

"She's sick," Rick said. As the phone stopped, dead, in the middle of a ring. "We need to get her to her ship. And we've got to hurry – there's someone coming. Someone dangerous. *Let's go!*"

But by then it was already too late.

Because two dozen Space Pirates stood in the door.

Space Pirates.

Walt Fulton was so sick of Space Pirates he could just scream. When he saw them he wanted to pull out his blaster and blow them all to kingdom come, but he didn't have a blaster and there wasn't time, anyway, he had to get Lena back to her Space ship before, before –

Lena screamed.

The Space Pirates barged right on in to the apartment, not even bothering to knock or ask a by your leave, nothing, isn't that just like Space Pirates? They never wait to get an invitation.

And they didn't have to, anyway; the door hung broken from Rick Mitchell pounding it open.

I hate *Space Pirates,* Walt thought. He reached reflexively for his own blaster, but it wasn't there – the navy had taken it when it'd mustered him out of service.

"We've come for the queen," said the Space Pirates' captain. He had a blaster rifle in his arms, and as he spoke he leveled it at Walt. "You will give her to us now."

What on earth?

"Queen. . . ?"

The Space Pirate Captain scowled. "Stand aside, Walt Fulton," he said, "or you will die."

He gestured with his rifle like he meant business.

"Eat me," Walt Fulton said, and turned his back on the Space Pirate Captain as he stooped to lift Lena and carry her away –

Not a wise thing to do.

At all.

Turning his back on Space Pirates?

?

!

Insane, was what it was. But that was Walt Fulton for you, where it came to Space Pirates: he was brash, and in some ways he was senseless. He had a lot of nerve, and he was lucky, too.

Lucky enough to hear the hum that came from the Space Pirate Captain's blaster as he flipped the safety and got ready to blast Walt to kingdom come.

Lucky enough to catch the Pirate hard in the knees when he sprung half-blind and backward into him – Walt's shoulder caught the Pirate's knees and the Pirate's Alien backjointed balance went all akimbo, he came down beside Walt like a sack of rocks, disoriented, surprised, and Walt grabbed for the blaster.

Got it.

And came up shooting, *zam zam zam,* three fiery blasts of unforce that vaporized the heads off the three Space Pirates who'd been behind the Captain, the three who'd seen him roll and were trying to kill him, there were a dozen more behind those but they were disoriented now confused unlike the Captain coming up from his confusion trying to throttle Walt –

Zam!

But only for a moment before Walt put a skull-sized hole through his breastbone.

Zam! Zam!

Two more quick shots at the Pirate throng, and they were all running, now, running for their lives the idiots weren't worth nothing in a fight, that's Space Pirates for you, they think they're tough but it's all bluster, Space Pirate ain't worth a spit in space.

As Walt climbed to his feet, holding his new blaster-rifle with one hand, dusting off his jeans with the other. Saw Rick Mitchell standing there by Lena, gawking at him stupidly, *No need to gape, ape,* Walt didn't say, even though he wanted to. *Six years of commando hand-to-hand training and you could do the same. Easy if all you got to fight is Space Pirates; harder if you got to fight people used to working at the things they do.*

"Don't just stand there, Rick," he said. "We need to get her back to her ship."

Lena groaned, and Walt went to her side.

"What's the matter?" he asked. "Are you all right? Are you going to make it to the ship?"

She sucked in a breath. "Something wrong," she said. "I hurt so bad."

Her skin was green-white, waxy – she looked like a corpse. She groaned again, moaned long and low until the moan became a dirge.

The sound was piteous, bone-chilling.

"What can I do?" Walt asked.

Lena tried to answer, but the words stopped in her throat.

Rick was beside him, now, leaning in, staring into Lena's face. "Just get her to the ship," he said.

Lena was still changing. The more she changed, the more Walt recognized what she became. And the more he recognized the more he –

The more he saw her changed the more he felt disgusted. She was changing into – into something repugnant. She was going to change and change until she turned into someone he hated.

Walt knew that long before he admitted it to himself. But he felt it a long time before he knew that it was so.

I know her, Walt thought. They were words inside his head that he couldn't understand and didn't recognize. *She's out of sync with me in time.*

He didn't know why he thought that, but it felt very, very true.

"There isn't time to stare at her like that, Walt," Rick said. "We've got to go."

LIV

Rick drove them north to the spaceport in his tail-fin Chevy, that beautiful anachronic car so right and wrong both all at once, all the cars here in this weird Abductee place were out of time, a third of them had tail fins just like Rick's. Aliens abducted a shipload of them, someplace, must've been; God knew why they'd do that.

Or maybe He didn't. Lots of things about Space Aliens are hard to parse.

Rick drove along the oceanside, then inland to Lena's starship. He never asked for directions. Walt wondered about that when everything was over and he had all the time in creation to think about things that he regretted. And when he thought about it, it bothered him.

But it didn't bother him while it was happening. It just felt right, was all; Rick knowing everything about Lena's ship made a kind of sense that felt natural and easy.

Maybe it felt that way because of Lena.

Lena was a mess. There were great festering boils all over her, and more and more she looked like something Walt couldn't bring himself to touch.

But he held her anyway. Held her as she cried and trembled; held her as she pleaded to God begging not to die.

"I love you, Walt," she said. Over and over again. Walt told her that he loved her too, but the truth was that he wanted to run away and hide.

If you could ask him where she wouldn't hear he'd've said he didn't love her. Not one bit. He hardly even knew her, he'd've said; how could he love anyone like that?

But even that would have been a lie.

Because the opposite of love isn't hating, or wanting to run away because it hurts to see. The opposite of love is getting up and walking off because you just don't care. And Walt Fulton cared so hard he shook and trembled almost as violently as Lena did. He hurt so bad when he looked at her that he wanted to die, and maybe he could have done that one more time, but he didn't.

He kept going because he didn't have any choice.

He was here, this was what he had to face, and he faced it. He hurt too bad to do anything else.

LV

Space Pirates followed them the whole way out to the spaceport. Walt noticed them when they were about halfway up the coast, when he glanced through the back window to see them riding behind the Chevy on air cycles that looked almost like witches' brooms.

Walt expected them to overtake the car, but they never did. They held back, kept their distance even when they came to a stop a few feet from Lena's starship.

That was the first time Walt got a good look at it from the outside.

That was when he realized what the ship was.

Space Pirates.

He recognized the ship because he'd seen it before – in that awful place where no light shines, when the Space Pirates killed him and ate him alive.

But that just didn't make any sense.

No sense at all.

Because Walt already recognized what Lena was

changing into. And what he recognized was from a part of his life almost as divorced from the Space Pirates as it possibly could be.

Because Lena was metamorphosing into Krant.

Krant wasn't a Space Pirate. Or maybe she was but it didn't matter: Walt knew Krant from the Space Alien Navy. If she'd ever been a Space Pirate before that, Walt didn't know about it – and as far as he was concerned it didn't matter. She was the grossest Space Alien Walt had ever met. She was the phlegmy-ooky *thing* that'd found him in his grave and woke him back to life; the repulsive body-thief who'd stolen his DNA and made the daughter that he never knew and couldn't find.

Walt hated Krant. He always had, from the very first moment he'd set eyes on her. It wasn't in him to feel any different seeing Lena change into *that.*

I ought to give her to the Space Pirates, Walt thought. And hated himself for thinking so.

The Space Pirates kept their distance as Walt lifted Lena out of the back seat of the car and carried her to the ship. Walt was sure they'd attack as he stood dumbfounded trying to figure out how he was going to open the door, but they didn't. Maybe because the door opened itself the moment it approached it.

And slammed shut behind him the moment he was through.

Before Rick Mitchell could follow.

And maybe that was for the best.

LVI

Walt carried Lena who was Krant to the Resurrection machine where she'd saved his life the day before.

Saved his life the day before.

How can I hate her when she loves me so much?

But he hated her. He really did. He couldn't help himself.

When he reached the medical room he bent to set Lena in the resurrection machine. But before he could she woke just enough to warn him away.

She shook her head. "No," she said. "The resuscitator."

And she pointed at a device that was like no other Walt had ever seen.

What it looked like was a coffin.

An unfinished wooden coffin – the kind that desperate soldiers build for themselves before they go into battle.

He lifted her off the gleaming metal-and-ceramic bed of the resurrection machine, carried her across the room, and set her to rest in the coffin. In a moment the device whirred to life, glowing and humming; rumbling somewhere deep inside the wooden sides. In another Lena began to change again.

Or maybe it wasn't change at all, what happened in that box.

Maybe it was just a revelation.

Maybe the light that surrounded the box was a True Light.

Because the moment it surrounded Lena something fundamental about the nature of her appearance – *changed.*

One moment she was Lena metamorphosing – vaguely human, strangely Alien; more like a woman than a woman is like a man. A green cast creeping over her blue skin, but underneath that green she was blue and exotically alien. . . .

And then suddenly the blue was green.

Completely and entirely green. Just the telltale green that always stains the skin of Space Pirates. Some people say Space Pirates get that way from some strange chemical reaction that happens when their ships sail down onto the *River of Our Destiny.* Others say the green is a badge of honor, like a tattoo that all Space Pirates wear.

No one knows for sure. No one but the Space Pirates themselves.

"You're a Space Pirate," Walt said. "You lied to me."

Lena shuddered. She opened her eyes. She looked so . . . *sad.*

Wounded.

"I never did," she said. "You never asked."

Walt wanted to scream at her. Not because she was a Space Pirate; Walt didn't care about Space Pirates like that, even if he liked to fight with them. He wanted to scream because the thing she was becoming nauseated him, and made him tremble, too, and there was only one thing that ever made him feel that way.

And it wasn't just a revelation of the light, like Lena's suddenly Space Pirate green complexion. What made Walt feel sick with himself every time he looked at Lena was what she was metamorphosing into.

And that was Krant.

Krant.

Hideous, hideous Krant. Skin like tripe; eyes like pools of drooling eggs. Krant's spider-maw blistering out all around where Lena's mouth should be.

Lena looked at her hands, metamorphosing into snaky, squidlike things. "This isn't right," she said. "Something's broken."

"You never told me what you were," Walt said.

Lena looked at him. He wasn't sure if she looked ashamed or angry or cold or if she hated him the way all Space Pirates did because of who he was.

As a crack of thunder shook the walls.

"What the hell was that?"

Lena didn't know. But that didn't matter. Because the moment that he asked the question the room's far wall became a view-screen, and when it did they both could see the Space Pirates who surrounded the ship.

They were armed to the teeth with blaster rifles and Space Alien field artillery – big, big guns.

One of those guns had a faint glow around the barrel, as though it had just fired.

We are under attack, a voice said. That was the ship's voice, wasn't it? Walt thought that he remembered it, but he wasn't sure. *Defensive measures undertaken.*

The Space Pirate Captain stood before them on the screen, bruised and bloody, still defiant. He shook a fist at them.

"You are in my ship," he said. "I claim it as my heritage. You will submit to me, or you will die."

As the ship returned fire, big burning thunder sounds out of the gun bays just below the bridge, and now the ship's big hardened anti-osmotic fields came up – those fields were strong enough to keep out damn near anything, not just air and stones. They were strong enough to stop a megaton explosion from ground zero; they could be tuned to stop very literally anything, matter, energy, wave or particle: if the ship wanted it could stop all light reaching the ship from outside.

But the Space Alien Navy had tools for getting through even the hardest anti-osmotic field, and the big guns the Space Pirates had brought with them were Space Alien Navy stuff – Walt recognized the make and manufacture. They were only barely man-portable – a squad could carry one of those guns overland in pieces, but they'd all have backaches for days.

Must've towed 'em here behind those air scooters.

Not good. This was a planned attack, something deliberate. Not just another ad hoc attempt to consummate by abduction an impulsive Space Pirate design.

The ship was still firing – ten, maybe twenty rounds of force a minute. Those were Space Pirate numbers; big Navy guns couldn't let off more than half that number.

The Space Pirates had anti-osmotic fields up around each of their guns – no great trick, since the field generations are built into all Navy field artillery – so all the fire and the counterfire accomplished at first was fireworks, big white sheets of light along the fields for every round that hit home, and look, Lord, craters all around the guns, it was going to be a slag pit out there any moment now.

The Space Pirates were returning fire as good as they were getting, not so much because their guns could fire quickly as because they'd brought at least a half a dozen of them –

If the Space Pirates had planned this, they'd know about the ship's defenses, and damn likely would know how to get around them –

Damn.

Look at that.

There, at three o'clock – dirty little SOB in seeming retreat, easing away from the battle with his gun loaded but unaimed, and the idiot ship didn't realized *couldn't* realize that he was easing back for cover and a better shot, he was way down on the target list –

"Right there," Walt said. "All your fire on that one, right there. Take him out."

Disobeying, the ship said. *Order would allow serious threats time to regroup and focus fire –*

"Override, damn it!" Walt shouted. "Those sons of britches know your tactical software. They know damn well you'd read that way, and they're playing you deliberately. *Take that Pirate out!"*

Overridden, the ship said.

And for ninety seconds all six of the ship's big blasters concentrated on the idiot who'd been in tactical retreat. *Zam! Zam! Zam! Zam! Zam! Zam!,* till now the poor monster's anti-osmotic field overloaded –

– turned white as bright –

– and came asunder, vaporized into a flash of endless light.

"Got 'im!" Walt shouted, and found himself reaching for the firing controls, God he loved this part, a good fight with the Space Pirates, how could he have gone so long without it? "Where's the gunnery bay?" Walt asked. "I want to get my hands in this."

As the ship went back to its half-sequential firing, slowly steadily trying to reduce all targets. . . .

And the wall beside Walt folded down, and there were a joystick, three levers, and a small array of buttons.

Nothing at all like Navy controls. Walt wasn't sure what to do with them, well, no, that one, that button there at his left hand by itself, bright white against the rest that were all dingy grey, that was the fire button, no question. Others would be gun selection and targeting, maybe force level, too, it'd take a moment to figure which was which, but not much more.

Stole a glance at the view screen, and saw three white flashes in the lower left, like they were aiming at Rick's Chevy, poor Rick parked there just inside the anti-osmotic field, that wasn't anyplace he ought to be, poor man was going to have a coronary.

"I think they've found a weak spot in your anti-osmotic field," Walt said. "Notice how they're targeting that same spot, over and over? Not quite often enough to register on your reinforce counter? Better do something about that. They're setting you up for an overload – six, seven of those guns all at once, three rounds in a row. You won't have time to stop it."

Disobeying –

"Override, damn it. And don't give me any more nonsense, all right? You got an objection, make it. But can the insubordination."

Overriding. Reprogramming.

"That's it – what did you do, double shield strength in that quadrant?"

Triple.

"Good. Don't let them get a clue you're on to them; they won't get it on their own. Those guns don't have any mechanism for reading shield strength – I know because I spent six months servicing them before they let me into pilot school." He looked at the whole field of battle, surveying it slow and carefully, telling the ship to pan so that he could get a look at what the Space Pirates had put behind them, which wasn't anything to speak of. "Okay," he said at last, "I want you to shift your firing pattern. Be cagey about it, and don't let them get a clue what you're doing. They don't realize that I'm helping you, or they wouldn't be trying that stupid trick with the shields; I don't see any reason to let them know the mistake they're making." He pointed. "Those three ships, right there. You see them?

I want you to load all of your fire onto those three – still shooting in sequence, and now and then a shot someplace else to that they don't realize you've freed up some targets. Got it?"

Instructions understood. Obeying.

LVII

Lena metamorphosed quietly all the while that Walt and the spaceship fought the pirates. Walt could see her writhing at the periphery of his vision that whole time, and now and then he heard her moaning – long, slow, and high, she moaned a sound like some strange mongrel howling mournfully at the alien moon.

LVIII

The three big guns in the second quadrant went blue-white a minute and a half after the ship concentrated its fire on them. You know the way that is: the glow; the long slow hum that a deaf man could hear through the soles of his feet three miles off; and then the blast not quite atomic in nature as all molecular bonds within the anti-osmotic fields came loose and rolled asunder –

Not a pretty sight, what happens when blaster force overloads an AOF. Spacefarers don't like to talk about it; nobody wants to die that way.

There was a moment – when the third gun's blast subsided and the battlefield was quiet - a moment when Walt thought that it was going to end that way. The Space Pirates would see what they were up against; they'd know that they were outgunned and outmaneuvered; and they'd run for their lives the way Space Pirates most always do once they know that they are beaten.

But it didn't happen like that.

Oh, most of them broke and ran; almost all of them,

in fact.

But not the Captain who'd laid claim to the ship. Not for a second! He stepped out from the shelter of his field gun and its AOF, tossed away his sidearm, and drew an ancient cutlass from the scabbard on his belt.

A sword, for God's sake! An outsize butter knife! You'd think the man had taken battle for an invitation to a dinner –

And Walt started to laugh, but only for a moment before the Captain charged them and the ship's sirens began to wail.

WARNING! the ship shrilled. *This frigate's defenses do not shield it from the attack in progress.*

– as the Space Pirate Captain reached the anti-osmotic field that shielded the ship –

– and cut through it with his blade.

Didn't cut long or wide or in any permanent way. But pierced it, and followed through the piercing, pushing through the field at a dead run.

Kept going till he damn near ran into the tail-finned back of Rick Mitchell's car.

Poor Rick.

He'd cowered in the front seat of his car all the while the battle had raged six yards away from him. He wasn't suited to that kind of fight, and probably wouldn't ever be, and he surely wasn't fit to fight that blood-mad Space Pirate or his cutlass.

"Ship," Walt said. "Target the Space Pirate. Take him out."

Impossible, the ship responded. *This ship is not equipped with antipersonnel weapons. Use of artillery at close range would cause collateral damage to all concerned.*

"Damn," Walt said. "All right, I'll take care of it. See if you can do something to distract that son of a birch, though, would you? Rick hasn't got a clue what to do with him. If you don't distract him Rick won't last long enough for me to help him."

Walt wasn't planning a duel, or even a fair fight: what

he planned to do was come out with his rifle leveled and blasting, take the nasty little duck out like cleaning trenches with a shotgun, and damn his little knife to hell.

But it didn't quite work out like that.

Because the cutlass wasn't made of any ordinary metal, and the Space Pirate Captain had a special gift for using it. When Walt came out the door of the ship into that place with where the Space Pirate stood swearing at Rick Mitchell, where the sky shimmered impossibly (the ship was doing that, wasn't it, the ship had made the sky above them into a thing like mother of pearl, shimmering, blinding bright, Walt got queasy looking at it), Walt came down the ramp with his blaster drawn and blasting, *zam zam zam zam* and by then the Captain should have been dead already.

But he wasn't.

As Walt came down firing, the Space Pirate turned to face him, meeting each blast from Walt's rifle with the flat of his blade –

That should have turned the cutlass hot as fire, and made it impossible for the Captain to hold the thing. But it didn't happen like that at all; the blasts hit the blade and went reflecting off in every direction, into the air, into Rick's Chevy, up off the big hard anti-osmotic field the ship still held over them. Damn near into Walt, one time, and it would have killed him if he hadn't ducked.

There's no time for this, damn it, Walt thought. *I've got to get back to Lena.*

And Walt did the only thing he could think of – the same thing he done to that same Space Pirate back in Lena's apartment: he rushed him. Rifle sounding, over and over, firing so fast that the Space Pirate didn't have a chance to figure what was coming at him. Right at him, into him, and onto him, when he got close enough slamming the business end of the blaster into the pirate's wrist like it was a bayonet, the sword went flying and Walt would have blasted the little duck to kingdom come right there but that isn't safe, you know, blaster fire at close range is as likely to kill the one who fires as it is to kill the target, guns with bullets will always have their place, some people say.

Bowled the Space Pirate over. Pinned him to the ground. And beat him to a pulp.

With the butt of his rifle, till the sound of the rifle butt on the Space Pirate's bones began to get to him; then with his bare fists, till the ugly little duck quit trying to fight back.

"Get into the ship," Walt called to Rick Mitchell. "It isn't like we've got all day."

When Rick was half-way up the ramp Walt got up, lifted the Space Pirate Captain by his collar, and threw him ungently into the mother-of-pearl wall. And turned his back on him as he started back into the ship.

Bad idea, that.

Because the Space Pirate Captain was nothing if he wasn't determined: the moment that he came to rest at the base of the mother-of-pearl wall that was the ship's big hard anti-osmotic field, he was scrambling to his feet, bloody and battered but not beaten, running to get the sword Walt had tossed away so nonchalantly –

– retrieving it –

And charging at Walt's back.

If he'd been a moment quicker, Walt would have been in trouble. As it was he reached the top of the platform just barely in time to have the ship's door slam shut on his face.

LIX

Walt reached the bridge as Lena changed. What he saw when he got there wasn't what he expected – and it wasn't something he could cope with, either.

She's disgusting, Walt thought when he saw her. *Look at her, look at her.* He hated himself for thinking it, but there wasn't any denying what he saw.

She looked repugnant.

She was Krant, the monster of a Space Alien who'd swiped his DNA and made a daughter of him without ever asking his consent.

"You trapped me," Walt said. "You tricked me into this."

Krant who was Lena opened her eyes. Shook her phlegmy head. "I never did," she said, coldly. "I never could."

Walt felt dirty inside. Disgusted with himself. "Why?" he asked her. "What did I ever do to you?"

But he knew the answer to that. He could see it now, as he never couldn't've back when they'd both served in the Space Alien Navy: look at the green hue of her tripey flesh.

She's a Space Pirate.

Walt had done lots of bad to the Space Pirates. It wasn't any wonder that they'd set a curse like Krant upon him.

Krant shook her head again. "It isn't what you think," she said. "In our hearts we'll always love you."

Walt almost started to laugh – the only thing that stopped him was the queasy feeling in his stomach.

"That's stupid," he said. "You hate me. I hate you. You're Space Pirates, and I'm Walt Fulton."

"You're a hero," she said. "You always try to do what you think is right, no matter what it costs you. Of course we love you."

"But we're enemies!"

"Even so."

Walt turned away from her, watched lightning shimmer back and forth across the mother-of-pearl sky. He felt like, like – like somebody reached inside his head and turned him inside out.

Krant-Lena sat up in her coffin.

Grabbed his wrist.

Stopped him dead in his tracks.

She was strong enough to do it, too.

"I never let them kill you," she said. "I tried to make them stop."

Walt looked into her eyes. Ugly, ugly eyes, syrupy with phlegm. Each eye had a dozen yellowish pupils floating free like egg yolks in a bowl. "You're lying," he said. "You were there. I know you were. I remember now. I saw you when they pulled me from the cockpit."

She looked ashamed.

"I was." she said. "I'm sorry."

"You gnawed my bones," he said.

"I came to know you," she says. "I came to love you."

But he was sure she never did.

"You've got a plan. I want to know what it is."

Lena-Krant sobbed. She sounded so sad. Walt began to feel bad for her, which just made him more disgusted with himself.

"I could never tell you. I promise you I never would."

She stepped out of the coffin.

Crossed the room, opened the door, and walked out into the hall.

The far wall was lit up again, and now it showed the Space Pirate Captain trying to hack his way through the ship's fuselage with his sword. He wasn't getting anywhere, thank God.

Walt shook his head. Followed Lena down the corridor. She went straight toward the room that was the mirror of his secret heart – and opened the door across from it.

The security door.

The door into the worm hole.

She opened the door into a world that looked like hell waiting to engulf them – and stepped through.

"My home is yours," she said. "Treat her well."

As the door slammed shut behind her.

Walt tried to open it. He wanted to ask her what the hell she meant!

He wanted to know what she was doing, and where she was going, and, and –

But when opened the wormhole it was turned upon another place and time, and Walt Fulton looked through to see the blackest heart of space.

Deep, deep space black and starless as the place beyond creation.

LX

Walt waited for her to come back for a long time, but she never did.

After a long long while Rick Mitchell found him there, and asked him why he looked so sad, what's wrong, he asked, you look like death and dying, but Walt could never say.

Then they sat together waiting by the door until they both knew naught would ever come of it.

And gave up waiting.

And left the ship.

LXI

The Space Pirate Captain descended on Walt and Rick as they left the ship. "You're mine," he said, "I have you!"

For a moment Walt thought he was going to try to eat them alive.

Or pick them up and throw them half across the world.

But he didn't. He just stood there in front of them, sword in hand, looking belligerent and demanding, furious and bloodthirsty and right about to cry, too, all those things at the same time.

"Let me by," Walt said. "We don't have any business with you."

He looked so green, Walt thought. Was that something Space Pirates got from their parents, or something that came on them because they were pirates?

"The ship is *mine,* Walt Fulton. I claim it from you! I claim it as my right!"

"I don't care what you claim," Walt said. "Go bother someone else."

"I challenge you! Submit to me or die!"

Walt turned away from him. Started walking toward the city.

"Get away," he said. "Don't bother me."

As the Space Pirate raised his sword high overhead –

And lightning struck it, setting the Space Pirate afire.

When he finally stopped burning there was nothing left but ash.

LXII

Walt watched the fire, dumbfounded, the whole time it burned. When there was nothing left but bone and ember he stumbled to Rick Mitchell's Chevy and climbed into the passenger seat.

And sat there for the longest time.

Not thinking, not talking, not wondering why Rick didn't start the car and get them out of there. Not watching as the wind began to stir the Space Pirate's ashes, as it sifted them into the air and carried his remains away.

Hardly even breathing.

Just staring at the dashboard.

After a while he looked up and saw Rick Mitchell sitting beside him in the driver's seat.

"The Space Pirates," he said. "They got to you, didn't they?"

Rick laughed. "Where do you think you are?" he asked. "This whole damn world is crawling with 'em."

They both had a good laugh over that.

"I need a drink," Walt said. He knew that was a bad idea, drinking when he felt like he wanted to fall into a bottle and drown. But he hurt too much to do anything else.

"Yeah," Rick said. "Me too."

26997425R00086

Printed in Great Britain
by Amazon